THE LAND GRAB

The Legend of Big Heart · Book 1

Alfreda Beartrack-Algeo

7th GENERATION
Summertown, Tennessee

Library of Congress Cataloging-in-Publication Data
available upon request.

Cover and interior design: John Wincek

7th Generation
Book Publishing Company
PO Box 99
Summertown, TN 38483
888-260-8458
bookpubco.com
nativevoicesbooks.com

ISBN: 978-1-939053-40-4

27 26 25 24 23 22   1 2 3 4 5 6 7 8 9

Contents

Introduction

’m Alfred Swallow, and I’m eleven years old. The year is 1929, and I live with my nine-year-old brother, Elmer; my grandfather; my grandmother; and our mother. We live on the Kul Wicasa Lakota Reservation in Iron Nation, South Dakota. My brother and I used to live with our father and our mother in a two-story wood-frame house with the peeling gray paint two miles west of our grandparents’ cabin. All my friends would stop by after school for Karo syrup and fry bread. It was fun.

Everything changed last year when my father decided to leave for Cheyenne, Wyoming, to find work. He promised to write and send us money. My mother waited and waited, but he never came home. I knew he was dead because he would never abandon us. Tired of waiting and struggling, my mother, Elmer, Chepa, and I started living with our grandparents. Twelve moons have passed, and I still miss my house and my room, but most of all, I miss my father.

Even though we miss my father, our family is happy living a rustic life with traditional values. Little do I know just how much our traditional values will help me through rough times.

Lakota
New Year

It was the first day of spring and nature's new year. *Boom! Crack! Boom! Crack!* The thunder of colliding ice chunks that tumbled in the rushing water of the Missouri River was deafening.

I was excited to accompany my grandfather and my brother, Elmer, to the Missouri River for a water ceremony. I prepared well for the ceremony with my braided hair wrapped in otter skins. My center part and face were painted with sacred red-earth clay, and a golden eagle feather was tied to my scalp lock. A pair of hard-soled quilled deerskin moccasins adorned my feet. Grandfather let Chepa, my yellow Labrador, come with us. He romped through the tufts of new grass that lined the path as he looked for gophers.

I asked Grandfather, "May I paint Chepa with sacred red-earth clay?"

"No," he answered. "A dog is sacred and only painted for a special occasion, like for a sacred clown ceremony. Long before the horse came to our land, we depended on our dogs for many things. They carried our belongings across the prairies, played with our children and kept them safe, and warned us of danger. Once the horse arrived, everything changed. We became a horse nation of fierce warriors, ruling the great plains from north to south. We called the horse holy dog. The horse was much like our dogs—loyal, dependable, and resilient—but much faster."

A golden eagle swooped in front of us. "Kwit-kwit-kwit-kwit-kee-kee-kee-kee-ker." The eagle landed in a nearby tree and watched us.

Grandfather said, "Grandchild, the golden eagle is one of your spiritual helpers and came here to help you pray. At your birth, a golden eagle perched itself in a tree near the bedroom window where your mother was in labor, and it stayed there until you were born. It then flew away until he was only a dot in the sky. It is good it came to you today. Your time for transition into manhood is close. That is why you need to dream your spirit name."

"Why is it important for me to have a spirit name?" I asked.

Grandfather said, "Our spirits live in the spirit world long before we come to Earth as human beings. We all have spirit names in the spirit world. Often, on this human journey, we forget our spirit names. Dreaming helps us remember.

"A spirit name is vital because it will protect you. Alfred is not your spirit name. It was given to you in honor of a German doctor your parents were fond of. When your spirit dreams start, I will ask Pete Flying Crow to conduct a ceremony for you," Grandfather said.

How could I tell Grandfather that my spirit dreams already came to me every night? They showed me things that would soon happen, and sometimes they warned me about danger.

Like last month I had dreamed Junior White Hail ambushed me. The next day, I took a different path home from school, and I avoided getting beat up that day. My best friend, Orson, said Junior was mad and determined to beat me up, so he thought he should warn me to watch out.

Skirting from one side of the path to the other, I tried to avoid the mud puddles left over from the winter snowmelt. I was used to my thick socks and leather boots, so my tender feet felt every rock through my moccasins' rawhide soles.

"Ow!" Something poked me right through my left moccasin. It was a smooth, round black stone. When I picked it up, the stone throbbed in my hand like a beating heart. I put it in my coat pocket to show my friend Orson later.

When we reached the Missouri River, we saw the icy waves lapping against her shore. I thought Mother Nature chose her paints well today. Slivers of pink and lavender cut through the thick river fog like wildflowers on a vast Dakota prairie. The glow of the dawn colors reflected off the white bald eagle feather tied in my grandfather's long silver braids.

I could faintly hear Grandfather over the roar of the river as he handed me his elk-skinned drum.

"Grandchild, sing the four-directions song."

I knew the song well, since it was the first song I learned from my father.

Boom-boom. Boom-boom. The drumbeat resonated deep into the earth and bounced up into the heavens. Overhead, a chorus of squawking geese showered their blessings on us.

> Look toward the West.
> Your Grandfather is looking this way.
> Pray to Him, pray to Him! He is sitting there looking this way!
>
> Look toward the North.
> Your Grandfather is looking this way.
> Pray to Him, pray to Him! He is sitting there looking this way!

Look toward the East.
Your Grandfather is looking this way.
Pray to Him, pray to Him! He is sitting there
looking this way!

Look toward the South.
Your Grandfather is looking this way.
Pray to Him, pray to Him! He is sitting there
looking this way!

Look up above, upward.
God, the "Great Spirit," sits above us.
Pray to Him, pray to Him! He is sitting there
looking this way!

BOOM, boom, BOOM, boom.

Look toward the Earth.
Your Grandmother lies beneath us.
Pray to Her, pray to Her! She is lying there
listening to your prayers!

Grandfather motioned with his eagle fan to
each of the sacred directions and started his prayer:
"Great Spirit, Creator, hear my prayer and my
grandson's prayers today.

"We give gratitude to you, who embodies all
goodness and directs all things. We give gratitude
to our Mother Earth, who sustains and feeds us.
We give gratitude to the sun, moon, and stars
above. We give gratitude for water of life, our first
medicine. We give gratitude to the Missouri River

and all her creeks and streams. We give gratitude for this new season and the hope of rain and growth. We give gratitude to the water nations, the plant nations, the winged nations, the four-legged nations, and the two-legged nations. Lastly, we give gratitude for our traditional teachings you have taught us, and for Earth. We are all related."

Grandfather opened his porcupine-quilled bag. The wind wrapped the smell of dried traditional tobacco leaves around us. The sweet aromatic scent stung my nostrils.

"Grandchild Alfred and grandchild Elmer, take a pinch of tobacco from this bag and hold it in your right hand to make your offering prayer."

I reached into the bag and grabbed a small portion of dried tobacco. I handed that bag to Elmer, and he copied me. We shared our prayer with our tobacco offering and sprinkled it into the cold churning water of the Missouri River.

Grandfather handed me his porcupine-quilled bag and drum. As we walked home, I stayed behind him while he carried his eagle fan.

On our way home from the river, we passed by our uncle Jay's cabin. He was outside fixing a sagging clothesline. Uncle Jay was the youngest brother to my father. We waved at him, and Uncle Jay waved back. On impulse, I kicked up a few fancy steps and bellowed out a loud victory whoop. "Hoka Hey. Hoka Hey!"

I sheepishly shrugged my shoulders at the surprised look from Elmer and my grandfather.

"Well, I am just happy to see him," I said.

Grandfather's wrinkled eyes sparkled with amusement. "With a voice like that, you make a good camp crier."

When the red feed bin and oversized cottonwood tree near our house came into view, I exhaled a loud sigh of relief. My arms ached from the loose quills on the tobacco bag that poked me all the way home. The smell of buffalo stew and fresh Lakota fry bread made me forget my sore arms, and I thought only of my hungry stomach.

My grandmother stood on the porch, holding a tea towel. Her silver braids were tied in a coil under her black hairnet. She wore a clean white apron of starched muslin made from a flour sack.

"Come in, everyone, it is time to eat! Grandchild Alfred and Elmer, wash up and put your moccasins and ceremonial clothes away."

I dampened a few twigs of dried sage and wiped the wase from my head and face. My ceremonial clothes were carefully packed into a rawhide suitcase, and we placed them on the top shelf in my bedroom closet.

My extended family and I sat around the round kitchen table that my grandfather made for Grandmother many years ago. The oak table served as a centerpiece for meals. It was the table we used for homework, canning, sewing, drawing, painting, reading, and sitting around when welcoming friends and family. We shared many human emotions around this table. I always shared my stories and laughed along, pretending I was at ease, but I was not.

In my dream, I felt a sad wind blowing through my mind like a buffalo running against a storm. It was a strange storm, in a strange place, and all the things I ever wished for were stuck in the storm with me.

I wished I had the courage to tell Grandfather about my dreams, about the ghosts and spirits that came to me; I wished I had a spirit name; I wished I had a lot of friends like Orson; I wished I could stand up to that bully, Junior White Hail, even if it hurt; and I really wished my father hadn't left us.

I dreaded the nighttime and the dreams that sucked me into the portal beyond this world.

Walking in Two Worlds

The bright morning sunbeams were extra special today. They were shimmering like angels dancing down from the clouds. I put Chepa inside the fenced yard and joined my grandparents, who were patiently waiting in the high buckboard wagon seat. The wagon was hitched to Sally and Sadie, two gentle and trusting quarter horses.

It was Easter Sunday, and we were off on a short ride to attend services at the Messiah Episcopal Church. It was a humble one-room church that was heated by a woodstove located below in a small basement. Grandmother cradled in her lap a white lily plant in a red clay pot that she was donating for the church altar.

Within minutes of our arrival, the small church was packed shoulder to shoulder with community members. Seven long narrow windows spilled light across the wooden pews filled with hopeful faces. A sacramental gold chalice and plate and one lone white lily sat on top of a white-draped altar. Above the altar hung one of the most magnificent paintings I had ever seen. It was of a shepherd holding a baby lamb with his flock at his feet. I was captivated by the light in the painting and by the details and skill of the artist.

Bishop Roberts delivered the service in fluent Lakota. Although he was not Lakota, he knew the Lakota ways well. Sharing a hymnal, my grandparents beamed like children singing away their fears and worries. Harmonizing voices filled the church to the ceiling with Lakota hymns. I studied the ceiling. I wondered how long it would take for me to paint a sequence of stories, much like Michelangelo painted on the ceiling of the Sistine Chapel in the Vatican City of Rome.

Laughter pulled me out of my daydreams; it was Bishop Roberts telling funny stories in Lakota. Soon, the service was over.

The ride home in the wagon was bumpy and dusty.

I scooted closer to Grandmother and asked, "How did the Messiah church become as popular as our traditional ceremonies?"

Grandmother motioned with her hands across the horizon. "This is all our land, the land of the Seven Council Fires, or Seven Bands. Our band is the Sicangu Brule, Kul Wicasa Oyate. The government-to-government relationship between the Seven Council Fires and the United States government became strained and bloody. We were forcefully relocated several times until we ended up here, in this land. Our Chief, Solomon Iron Nation, sought to make peace with the United States government because he believed we could not survive against the influx of white soldiers. There were too many of them.

"Chief Iron Nation developed a friendship with an Episcopal priest named Father Luke Walker. Father Walker told Chief Iron Nation about a man called the Messiah from across the water. He said the Messiah lived long ago but his teachings lived today: humility, perseverance, respect, honor, love, sacrifice, truth, and compassion. He was killed for teaching the truth.

"Chief Iron Nation was impressed, because these were the same virtues as our Lakota people. He saw that the teachings of the Messiah could bring renewed hope to his people. Chief Iron Nation was influential in the building of the Messiah Episcopal Church in 1884. He attended services as much as possible until his passing in 1894. Chief Iron Nation was one of our first Lakota chiefs to be buried under the earth in a grave and not placed above the earth on a traditional scaffold."

Grandmother patted my hand. "You see, grandchild, when we go inside our church house, we feel renewed faith from the words and the songs shared inside the church house."

I nodded up at Grandmother, not quite understanding the entire concept of walking in two worlds, but the radiance in her face was comforting. I was quiet the rest of the ride home, listening to my grandparents still chuckling over the funny stories they heard at church.

When we arrived home, I unhitched Sally and Sadie, put them out to pasture, and decided to go fishing.

I told my mother, "Chepa and I are going to Medicine Creek to catch some fish for supper tonight."

Grabbing my coat and fishing pole, I pushed a tin can filled with earthworms down into my pocket. I decided today I would go as far back up the creek as I could, maybe catch some big catfish.

Oops! I almost forgot my worn green canvas tote bag, packed with an ample supply of dried deer pemmican, water, and of course my sketch pad and charcoal sticks. I turned around, grabbed the bag from behind the door, and hoisted it over my shoulder. Then down the road we went.

Whew, it sure will be nice to be alone for a change.

The smell of damp earth let me know we were close to the creek. A flight of swallows swept through the dense treetops. I rarely came this deep into Medicine Creek woods. I found an ideal spot on the grassy bank. I baited my line with a worm and threw the line into the calm water. Chepa ran off to explore.

I looked around for something interesting to draw. My eyes spotted an old gray cedar tree with peeling bark, twisted into the ground. *Aww, the perfect subject.*

I picked up my sketch pad and charcoal sticks and jumped right into my drawing. Halfway through my drawing, I heard a high-pitched bark. I looked around, but since I couldn't see anything, I went back to drawing. Next, a strong movement in my coat pocket made me think that a runaway earthworm had frantically tried to escape. I put my sketch pad and charcoal down. I reached into my pocket, expecting to feel a mucky earthworm slipping through my fingers . . . but no, it was the round black stone that I had found at the Missouri River.

The stone turned warm and moved from side to side in my hand. I wondered, *Am I dreaming this? Is this stone trying to warn me?*

An eerie stillness filled the woods: no birds singing, no crickets, no frogs, nothing but silence.

I slipped the stone back into my coat pocket and stood up.

"Grrrrr. Grrrrr."

I wanted to run, but fear had frozen my feet in place; I couldn't move an inch. A gray wolf appeared next to the twisted cedar tree I was drawing. She was baring her teeth. I recognized the noise; it was the yapping of wolf pups. Her den was probably near the cedar tree. I caught a movement in the corner of my eye; two growling wolves joined the first wolf. The three wolves, defending their territory, stood with erect ears pointed forward and tails held ready for action.

I knew I needed to leave fast. I figured I could easily back away unharmed if I went slow and did not anger them. I slid my shaking hand downward and picked up a piece of driftwood as I slowly stepped backward.

"Woof. Woof." Chepa appeared out of nowhere and lunged out in front of me.

"No, Chepa. No!" I shouted. "Come here! Now!"

I grabbed his collar to hold him still. Too late! Chepa broke free from my grip and headed straight toward the wolves. The wolves, riled up by Chepa's barking, charged back toward us.

I swung my driftwood club at the head of the wolf leading the pack. It was the alpha male.

A deep, sickening thud told me I hit my mark. The male wolf yelped and rolled to the ground. I retrieved my pocketknife from my pants pocket and snapped it open. The alpha wolf regained his footing and ran back at me. He jumped; his heavy weight was on top of me. I could smell the rancid bacteria in his breath from his last meal.

I heard Chepa yelp in pain, and I knew he was in big trouble. Glancing in his direction, all I could see was a big ball of gray and yellow fur with fangs . . . rolling over and over.

The alpha male sank his teeth deep into my right thigh and yanked a piece of flesh out. Unbearable pain seared through my entire body. I managed to stab him in the leg. He yelped and retreated back a few feet, but he was still in his attack posture with ears forward.

My lungs were on fire. I swung the driftwood club with all the strength I could muster. The alpha male wolf went down, hurt but still alive. He stood up, this time with his ears pinned back and his tail tucked between his legs. He retreated back toward the den, and the other two wolves followed him.

Chepa lay limp in the grass, bleeding and helpless. He tried to raise his head when I called him, but he was too weak. Tears ran down my face. Chepa was my best friend, even better than Orson.

"Chepa, please don't die. I will get you home. I promise."

I knew we had to move soon because the wolves would be back, and maybe with more pack members. I also knew that I was unable to carry Chepa home on my back in my condition. I'd lost a lot of blood, and my leg was swelling fast.

I put my head on Chepa's heaving chest, and I prayed. "Great Spirit, please help me. I know I have not always been the best person, but please help Chepa. He is a good dog. He saved my life."

"Son, you must get up!"

I sat up. It was the voice of my father. But it wasn't my father.

In front of me stood the biggest golden eagle with the most intense yellow eyes I had ever seen. He had a dried dogwood tree limb in his sharp talons. He dropped the limb at my feet and flew off toward the woods. I couldn't believe my eyes. The eagle returned with another limb, and yet another, until there was a pile of tree limbs in front of me. The eagle flew away just as quickly as he had appeared.

The story my grandfather told me last week filled my thoughts: *"Grandchild, a golden eagle came to your mother when you were born. It will surely watch over you throughout your life."*

My instincts told me that this was the same golden eagle. My father sent him to help me survive.

Time was short; I had to act fast. I struggled to stand, but I did it! I was upright and determined. I spotted a patch of reeds and cattails nearby. Grabbing one of the straighter limbs, I used it as a cane to brace my body. Picking up my pocket-knife from the bloody grass, I wiped it clean and proceeded to cut the reeds until I had a small pile.

Fingers turning and twisting the grass into a rope paid off. I had enough to get the job done and went to work tying the tree limbs together. It seemed like an eternity, but I finally finished the dogwood travois that would transport Chepa home.

Chepa's eyes were rolled back in pain, and I could hear his faint whimpers. I moved him onto the Y-shaped travois and placed my canvas pack and fishing pole on top. I locked my shaky arms under the narrow top of the travois and started the long trek homeward.

I fought for every footstep through the tall grass. The wooden sled carrying Chepa home grew heavier by the minute. The silhouette of my grandparents' cabin against the setting sun let me know we were almost there. A vague memory of Grandfather running toward me stuck in my head. I could see his mouth moving, but I couldn't hear his words because of a buzzing in my head. Everything was spinning around and around. The familiar hand I feared in my dreams reached out of the darkness and pulled me into the void of nothingness.

Partners on the Mend

When my eyelids fluttered open, it took me a moment to remember where I was. My first thought was *Chepa! Where is Chepa?*

A warm wet tongue licked my hand, and I turned my head and looked into Chepa's puzzled face. A gash from his left eye to his nose was sewn closed. He rocked the bed with his wagging tail, happy to see me awake.

Everything started coming back to me. I remembered the fight with the wolves and the gashes on my thigh and arm. I looked down at my thin legs and arms and realized I must have been sick for a while. The memory of it all left a bitter taste in my throat. I swallowed to get rid of the taste, but it stayed.

Like on Chepa, stitches zigzagged up my forearm like a lightning bolt. Grandmother had quite the knack for stitching wounds and treating injured people and animals with her traditional herbal-medicine ways. I felt fortunate that my grandparents still carried on our traditional healing practices even though they had to hide them from Superintendent O'Neil and the other government officials.

After a painful scoot to the edge of the bed, I slowly slid my feet over the edge and onto the woolen rug below. The wood floor creaked as I balanced my weight. Chepa jumped down right behind me, ready for action.

I noticed my right leg was wrapped in muslin cloth.

"Whew," I said out loud.

My mind was back to normal, but my body was still very weak. I knew I should take it slow and easy, but that was not my style.

Yearning for fresh air and sunshine, I listened carefully for any sounds from the other rooms, and I realized the cabin was empty. Glad to see my walking stick leaning up against the wall, I limped out of my room, past the kitchen table, and down the back porch steps.

"Alfred, get back inside!" Mother caught me and shooed me right back in the house.

She said, "Maybe you can go outside tomorrow, but today you need to stay inside and rest. You've spent an entire week in bed recovering from the wolf attack and you are still very weak."

Shucks! Disappointed and anxious, I headed back inside. I was out of drawing pencils, so I decided to catch up on homework. I was grateful that Chepa and I survived the wolf attack. I knew missing a week of school meant a lot of catching up. After digging around on my dresser for a pencil, I found two drawing pencils and a box of charcoal. *Yes!* I could do homework later.

The day passed fast, and I finished the last of my traditional medicine tea. I must have dozed off, because a loud ruckus from the chicken coop woke me up.

I slipped on my moccasins and stepped out onto the back porch. Grandfather was already there, holding a lit lantern and ready to investigate. I surprised him.

"Grandchild," he said, "how are you feeling?"

I replied, "I am much better. Shall we go check the damage?"

"Sure, let's go," Grandfather said.

I about lost my balance when something skirted past us and disappeared out the back of the coop. After the wolf incident, I was a little edgy. The orange glow of our lantern spilled across a pile of white chicken feathers and a carcass of a half-eaten hen. Eggs were scattered everywhere across the coop floor. We decided to wait until daylight to get a better look.

I told Grandfather, "When it gets light, I will come back to get a better look. For now, let's cover the hole in the chicken wire with a board."

Still taking it easy the next morning, after breakfast I went to work fixing the chicken coop while Grandfather and Elmer went to check on two heifers ready to give birth. I watched Elmer, his sleeves rolled up, walk with Grandfather to the barn. By his posture, he was feeling mighty important.

I could see so much of myself in my little brother. I remembered my grueling years during calving season; I was seven years old when Grandfather and Father put me on watch patrol, which meant I watched the cows and heifers for hours. I looked for any sign of birthing problems. The truth was, in the beginning I did not know what I was watching for. Now, I could spot a cow or heifer in distress a mile away. I knew with Elmer's enthusiasm he would learn fast too.

Grabbing a can of nails and my homemade rock hammer, I headed toward the chicken coop.

Right off, I found a small patch of red fur stuck around the opening of the hole in the chicken wire. Determined to put a stop to the egg thief, I started by doubling up on the chicken wire and reinforcing the skirting around the bottom of the coop.

After a good hour of steady piecemealing and nail pounding, I needed a rest.

I plopped down in the shade next to my boss-dog, Chepa. Just like me, Chepa was still on the mend.

"Woof. Woof." Chepa jumped to attention.

I looked toward the main road. It was my next best friend, Orson High Elk, waving and carrying on to get my attention.

"Hau, friend. Are you busy? You got a minute?" he hollered through his cupped hands.

I hollered back. "Taking a break. Come on over!"

Orson cleared the barbwire fence effortlessly. Although we were the same age, Orson was one inch taller than me and had much longer legs. He squatted down next to me and rubbed Chepa's ears. Chepa jumped on Orson and sniffed his pockets.

Orson said, "I heard about what happened with the wolf. So sorry, but so happy you and Chepa are okay. Look! I brought you both a treat today. Some fresh dried deer jerky."

Chepa, upon hearing his name, stood at attention in front of Orson. Orson handed him a big piece of jerky, and he disappeared behind the nearest brush, savoring his treat. Orson and I then shared the other jerky over a good visit.

I always enjoyed talking with Orson. He made me laugh a lot, no matter how bad things were. Orson moved here with his family from the Rosebud Reservation, and we had been friends since.

Orson reached over and yanked my braid. "Friend, I like your long braids. I cannot wait for my hair to grow long again so I can wear my hair braided."

I teased Orson. "Yeah, and all the girls will chase you around the schoolyard just to touch your braids."

Orson laughed. "Friend, if I didn't feel so sorry for you right now, I would wrestle you to the ground and make you beg."

I swung at him with my walking stick, but he was too fast. Our horseplay toned down when we noticed Grandfather keenly watching us from the barn. I knew he was instructed by Grandmother to keep an eye on the stitches in my thigh and forearm.

Orson said, "Come on, friend, I will help you finish this project."

I held the boards against the skirting while Orson pounded the nails in one by one. We finished up in no time at all and took a water break.

Orson asked me, "Is Junior White Hail still harassing you?"

Embarrassed by my answer, I said, "Yes, he is. He chased me home from school two weeks ago. Geez, I wish he would move back to Lower Brule Agency."

Orson said, "Yes, I know what you mean. None of us likes how he treats you. It always seems to happen when I am not around. I am sure he will eventually grow tired of being a bully and grow up."

Deep down, I knew better. Junior White Hail was not going to stop until he beat me up bad to prove he was bigger and tougher. I shivered at the thought. I tried not to let Orson see my fear.

Saved by the moment—the barn door flew open, and Elmer shot out like an arrow on a mission. He ran toward us, shouting, "Alfred! Orson! Remember Belle, the white-faced heifer? She just had twins!"

Elmer rambled on. "You should have seen me help them be born. Grandfather said I did a great job."

Orson and I responded at the same time: "Good, Elmer. That is good."

Orson looked up at the midday sun. "It is getting late, my friend. I need to get home and cut firewood. Will you be at school tomorrow?"

"Yes."

I watched Orson clear the fence and noticed a cloud of dust coming down the road. Elmer asked, "Alfred, what are you looking at?"

"That cloud of dust on the road is coming to our house. Little brother, quickly go tell Grandfather."

I walked toward the front yard to get a better look as a black Model T pulled into the driveway. Chepa, sensing danger, ran around the house in a frenzy of howls and barks.

Chepa's warning, as well as the sick feeling in my gut, told me this visitor was dangerous and could not be trusted.

Twisted Words

C hepa! Stop!" I shouted. "Come here."
I caught him and tied him to the porch rail
while Grandfather and Grandmother came out to
the front porch. Both of them had an idea of who
would step out of that fancy car: Mr. Jim O'Neil,
the superintendent for our Lower Brule Agency. He
was wearing a brown pinstriped suit, and he had a
tattered black leather briefcase tucked tightly under
his arm. He blew his nose into a white handkerchief
and started up the walkway toward us.

Grandfather greeted him at the porch steps.
"Good day, Superintendent O'Neil. What brings
you out this way on a dusty Sunday afternoon?"

Snorting and coughing out road dust, he
answered, "I figured it was time to talk business with
you and Lucille—that is, if you have a few minutes."

Grandfather smiled. "Sure, come on in. The
coffee is fresh, and we just pulled a hot apple pie
out of the oven."

Superintendent O'Neil walked by. Elmer and I nodded at him, but he just stuck his nose in the air and pretended not to see us.

Grandmother silently pointed us, with her mouth, to the porch bench—a gesture that told us to stay put until Superintendent O'Neil was finished with his business.

I idly sat strumming my fingers and watching tumbleweed dance in the dry whistling wind. Not able to stand it any longer, I inched my way toward the window until I could see inside without being obvious. I could vaguely hear the rise and fall of their conversation inside. I pressed my nose up against the window to get a better look.

I whispered to Elmer, "They are sitting around the kitchen table eating. Mother is serving Superintendent O'Neil apple pie and coffee."

I whispered, "Superintendent O'Neil has bulging eyes!"

His eyes were following every move our mother made around the kitchen table. It made my stomach turn. When I was confined to bed after the wolf attack last week, I heard my mother and grandmother talking in the kitchen. Although they both whispered, I could hear every word. Mother said she thought Mr. O'Neil was sweet on her. He told her she needed a good man to take care of her and her two sons. He said that my father was worthless and stupid for leaving his family behind. That my father would never come back to Iron Nation.

Superintendent O'Neil's words were cruel and untrue. I knew my father would come back someday, because I would find him and bring him home.

I said to Elmer, "Superintendent O'Neil is pushing his plate away."

"Mr. and Mrs. Plenty Buffalo," began Superintendent O'Neil, "as you know, we are in a drought, and it does not look like it is going to end anytime soon. Many of your neighbors are selling their land and moving into town or back to the agency. Without hay to feed their livestock, I am sure they have no choice in the matter. I have come here to offer you a good price for your land. It would be in your best interest to accept my offer because I am willing to give you a fair price: fifty-six cents an acre for your six hundred and forty acres along the river bottom."

From what I could see and hear, Superintendent O'Neil was not noticing the cold stares from Grandfather and Grandmother and continued on talking a mile a minute.

"I would ask Jess Miller to help us out and plow up the soil. Maybe plant some Russian olives and Chinese elm trees as a windbreak. Of course, Mr. Plenty Buffalo, this will only benefit you if . . ."

When the door opened and we heard the sound of a scraping chair on the wood floor, we figured Grandfather had had enough.

"Our land is not for sale. Three hundred and twenty acres of that land belong to my grandsons Alfred and Elmer. It is their allotted land, and someday they might want to own livestock and raise a family. What you are proposing is illegal, and it is sure not a fair price for river bottom land. You know as well as I do that plowing the native grass under and planting nonindigenous crops in the middle of a drought is not a wise move. I maintain the native grass on my land. I will not let you or Jess Miller plow our land up. I do not like your business proposal one bit! Please leave immediately!"

Closing his briefcase, Superintendent O'Neil narrowed his eyes, and his expression turned sour. "I understand how you feel, Mr. Plenty Buffalo. But with the financial markets failing, I believe this is a fair price. If I cannot get your cooperation, I will use the power vested in my position to take your land with or without your consent." As he tipped his hat to my mother, beads of nervous sweat rolled down his forehead. "Have a good day, folks. I will see myself out."

Tap-tap. Tap-tap. His angry shoes marched across the front porch and down the steps toward his vehicle. Superintendent O'Neil walked past me and Elmer. Anger was written on his face.

As soon as Superintendent O'Neil pulled away, I ran into the kitchen.

"Grandfather, is Superintendent O'Neil going to take our land away?"

Grandfather's face was flushed with emotion. "Grandchild, I have a lot to think about. We will talk later."

I looked at his large wrinkled brown hands, twisted from many years of hard work. I could not imagine my grandfather doing anything else in his life besides working the land he loved.

The silence in the room was deafening.

Grandmother picked up a bleached mussel shell to fill with cedar, sweetgrass, and sage. She struck a wooden match to the sacred herbs. A small blue flame ignited the mixture and filled the silence with cleansing smoke. Grandmother fanned us and the room with her eagle feather. The smoke curled and coiled and chased Superintendent O'Neil's words out the door behind him.

I decided I would conjure up a dream that would show me how to stop Superintendent O'Neil's crooked scheme. *Maybe I should tell Orson and my other friends,* I thought. *They might have a good idea what I can do to help Grandfather.*

A strong gusty wind blew grit and dirt right smack into my face. I glanced toward the west and saw a huge black cloud rolling toward us. *Horse feathers!* Another dust storm was rearing its ugly head! It was growing bigger and darker by the minute.

Shouting over the noise, I told Elmer, "Quickly, go help Grandmother and Mother close all the windows and light the kerosene lamps. The storm will be here soon!"

I found Grandfather in the corral. He had stopped fixing the fence post he was working on and was already preparing for a lockdown.

Grandfather hollered at me over the whistling wind. "Check the chicken coop and cellar doors. I will check the barn and grain bin."

It did not take long before we were inside safe and sound. I hung the wool army blanket over the back door, and we were ready to ride the dust blizzard out. The flames from the kerosene lamps flickered and illuminated the fine brown silt floating in the air. The day had taken a radical turn in more ways than one.

Chocolate Cake
in a Napkin

I t was exciting to start back to school. Today was the second Monday of the month, our spelling bee day. All last month I wore a gold paper star at school all day, pinned to my cotton shirt, because I spelled all the words correctly. I was determined to win the spelling bee today.

It was slow going with my walking stick. I still had another week before my sutures came out. Orson joined us in front of his house, and we walked the rest of the way to school together, laughing and joking.

Our school, Iron Nation Day School, was a one-room building with a wooden flagpole in the front yard. Inside, a cast-iron woodstove sat in the back of the room with a stack of wood nearby on the floor.

My desk and the other ten desks were neatly lined up in two rows facing forward. Orson; Junior White Hail; Ben Two Crow; Davis Two Crow; and the twins, Todd and Tim Yellow Hat, sat in the row next to the wall. The girls—Elizabeth Medicine Rattle, Lilly Blue Bird, Beatrice Holy Road, and Margaret Cloud Looking—sat in the row nearest the door.

Elmer and the other three younger students sat in the front of the classroom near Mrs. Red Feather's desk. Mrs. Red Feather had been my teacher since I was eight years old.

Mrs. Red Feather assigned us our school chores at the beginning of the school year last fall. My chore was to keep the walkway shoveled and clean. Orson's chore was to chop firewood and keep it stacked inside near the woodstove. Elmer's chore was to keep the blackboard clean and the chalk box filled.

Since we were usually the first students at school in the morning, Orson and I would take turns making the morning fire. The potbellied woodstove was hard to maintain. A couple of times last winter, I accidentally over-stoked the woodstove, and the room grew too hot for us. I had to open the door until it cooled down.

During the coldest days, Elmer and I carried two hot half-baked potatoes each in our pockets on our walk to school. The hot potatoes kept our hands from freezing. Once we were at school, we put our half-baked potatoes on top of the woodstove. By lunchtime they were fully baked and ready to eat. Delicious.

Mrs. Red Feather announced, "We will move the spelling bee to next Monday."

We all groaned. "Aww, shucks."

Mrs. Red Feather continued. "I decided we will have a special treat this afternoon. It will be a good way to welcome Alfred back to school."

"Good!" My voice led the chorus of rowdy boys.

I liked Mrs. Red Feather a lot, since she had a way of making her students feel special. Today, I was the special student.

We pushed the desks to the wall and made room to play games like Simon Says and Red Rover with the younger kids, but the boys ended up playing marbles, and the girls ended up drawing or creating paper clothes for their cardboard paper dolls.

At the end of the school day, I was just finishing a piece of chocolate cake that I held on a napkin when Mrs. Red Feather handed me a letter.

"Alfred, please give this to your mother. It is great news. We heard back from the Art Institute of Chicago regarding the scholarship application you sent them, and you have been selected! The scholarship board needs your mother's approval before they can release the funds."

I was thrilled. Stuffing the letter deep into my coat pocket, I turned my attention toward the wooden school door. Beatrice Holy Road led the way. The door flew open, and sunlight streamed across the floor. A flurry of excited and chattering students poured out onto the schoolyard.

When I walked out the door, Junior White Hail was waiting, and he knuckled my head as I went by. I glared at his broad shoulders, thinking, *Someday I am going to stand up and surprise the dickens out of you.*

I squinted in the bright afternoon glare, looking for a familiar yellow shape. There he was! I spied Chepa, lying in his usual spot in a patch of overgrown weeds near the flagpole.

"Woot. Woo." The sound vibrated through my cupped hands.

Chepa bounced up the steps, ready for action. Catching Elmer's eye, I motioned to him to meet me near the gate. He threw me a thumbs-up.

Orson was perched on the wooden bench by the school gate, talking with Elizabeth Medicine Rattle. Elizabeth moved here last summer with her family from Standing Rock, North Dakota. Orson seemed to be the welcoming party chairman for every new girl in school. He was in full theatrical mode, smiling and talking with his hands, obviously in the middle of a good story.

I decided to do my "prairie chicken sneak-up" routine. I walked up behind Orson and nudged him in the side as I moved my folded arms up and down like a chicken and danced bent-over in a circle, saying, "Cluck-cluck, cluck, cluck."

We all laughed except Orson, who jumped into a warrior pose. "Hey, be careful, old friend. If you weren't so wounded, I would wrestle you to the ground and make you plead for mercy."

I thought he was just showing off in front of Elizabeth, so I changed the subject.

"Are you going turkey hunting with me tomorrow?" I asked him.

"Heck yeah, what time?" Orson loved hunting more than he loved girls, and he was a good shot too.

"Crack of dawn at my house. I'll bring my Winchester twenty-gauge shotgun."

"Great plan. I'll bring my dad's Marlin rifle and some of my mother's pemmican."

Orson's full attention was on hunting, and Elizabeth did not like it one bit. Her mouth hung open, and her dark eyes glared at the back of Orson's head.

When he turned around and noticed the look on her face, he made it obvious with a nod that he wanted me and Elmer to disappear.

I winked at Orson. "See you later."

On the way home I told Elmer, "With that silly grin and glint in his eye, I think Orson likes Elizabeth a whole lot more than he is letting on."

Elmer looked dumbfounded and said, "I wonder why he likes her so much. She doesn't like fishing or hunting. She doesn't even like playing stickball!"

I was sure my little brother would understand in a few years.

It didn't take long for Elmer to start pestering me. "Please, Alfred, may I go hunting with you and Orson tomorrow? Please?"

"No, you're too young. Besides, you do not have a hunting rifle or a protection ceremony yet."

Elmer slumped his small shoulders forward and slowed to a snail's pace. "Please, big brother, please . . ."

I put my arm around my little brother and told him, "I paid down on a new hunting rifle at the Hickey's hardware store in Reliance. I should have it paid off by September, just in time for deer-hunting season. I will give you my old rifle and take you hunting then. Grandfather will fix you a medicine bundle to wear around your neck that will protect you while you hunt."

Satisfied by my response, Elmer squared his shoulders and picked up his pace.

I was glad he was happy. I knew he would become a good hunter someday. I noticed since our father left us that he did not like to be alone. Plus, he had become extra clingy after Superintendent O'Neil threatened to take our land and our home. I understood, because I had the same fears. Neither one of us wanted to be homeless again.

Our grandparents' house was visible in the distance, so on impulse, I raced past Elmer at full speed.

"Home or bust. Run, slowpoke! I will beat you to the front gate!"

Even with a lame leg, I was in the lead. That was, of course, until Chepa passed me at the last turn, leaving us in the dust. Out of breath, we reach the front yard together. Chepa was already there, licking his paws and yawning.

I ran up onto the porch and into the house to give my mother Mrs. Red Feather's letter.

She looked at me, surprised. "I hope this is good."

"It is! While you read it," I said excitedly, "I'll go to the well and fetch some fresh water for you."

As I ran toward the well, I noticed something on the hill above our cabin. Squinting out the sun, I could see it was two men, both holding rifles pointed at me. One of the men wore a straw hat and looked like Jess Miller. They made sure I saw them pointing their rifles. With shaking legs, I carried the water to the back porch. I tried to convince myself that they were just out hunting and meant no harm to me or the family, but my gut told a different story.

Dreamscape to Artscape

Grandfather sat on the front porch swing, tapping a beat on his leg and humming a prayer song. He stopped when he saw me and patted the empty space beside him. "Sit down, grandchild. I can tell something is on your mind. What is it?"

"There are two men on horseback on the hill behind us. I think one of them is Jess Miller, the rancher that is working with Superintendent O'Neil. They have rifles, and I think they are watching us."

"Probably just a few hunters looking for grouse," Grandfather said.

I nodded. But I felt unsettled.

I decided to change the subject. "Do you remember last fall when I carved a buffalo out of soap? And when Mrs. Red Feather helped me mail the sculpture along with a scholarship application to the Art Institute of Chicago? Today Mrs. Red Feather sent a letter home with me addressed to my mother. Mrs. Red Feather said I have been selected for the art scholarship, but only if my mother agrees, and I am worried she might not agree."

Grandfather smiled. "Congratulations, grand-child. I think it is a wonderful opportunity. Don't worry, I am sure your mother will support you wholeheartedly."

I was ecstatic because I loved art more than anything in the world, and it was one of my secret wishes to be a famous artist someday.

"Also, Mrs. Red Feather asked me to give this newspaper article to you," I said. "It is from the *Omaha World Herald* in Nebraska. The article reports that numerous clouds of grasshoppers have infested farm fields in Nebraska. Mrs. Red Feather thinks we are at risk of having the same problem here in South Dakota this coming summer."

"Put it on the table, and I will show Grandmother later," Grandfather responded. "She is a far better reader than me."

Before I forgot, I asked, "Is it okay if Orson and I go wild turkey hunting this weekend?"

"No walking, grandchild," said Grandfather. "Take your horse, Anpo, and stay away from the creek bend and far away from the wolf den. Chepa will need to stay home."

Grandfather swung his braids back and leaned forward. "Better get that thirty-pound ornery gobbler I missed last year. He is out there waiting. Biggest wild turkey I ever seen. I shot at him with my last shell and missed. That old turkey just walked away without a worry because he knew I was out of ammo. I'm surprised he didn't give me a good chase just for the heck of it."

Grandfather and I chuckled at the thought.

"I'm a darn good shot," I said, "so you can count on me to bring home that old gobbler, plus an extra turkey to salt and hang for later."

Grandfather reminded me, "One turkey is enough. Remember, we should only take what we need and no more. When we need another turkey, it will be there for us."

Hearing the whinny of horses, we looked up to see Jess and the other man slowly riding by. Grandfather waved at them, but they ignored him. They turned the horses around in our yard and headed off in the direction of Lower Brule Agency. The same terrible feeling I felt earlier when I was fetching water swept over me. I was sure Grandfather sensed it too, but he gave me his best reassuring smile.

"Suppertime! Come and eat," Mother called, and I thought, *What good timing*. I was so hungry no one had to call me twice.

The smell of fresh cornbread, northern bean soup with wild onions, and fried deer meat filled the cabin. The comforting aroma pushed my worry far away, at least for the moment.

As usual, I was the first one at the table. After the rest of the family found their seats, we sat quietly until Grandfather finished his prayer. Mother put a small pinch of food and a few drops of water into a wooden bowl; it was an offering for the spirits. After the blessing prayer, she placed it outside, and everyone was served. Dishes clinked with happy notes, and the room buzzed with good conversation and laughter.

After supper we sat by the woodstove and caught up on the day's events.

My mother said, "Alfred, my son, I am happy that all your hard work paid off and you have finally been awarded this art scholarship. Please know, you have my blessing. I will stop by the schoolhouse tomorrow and talk to Mrs. Red Feather and let her know as well."

My heart swelled seeing the proud smiles of my family.

After reading the news article Mrs. Red Feather had sent them, Grandmother said, "Oh dear, what will we ever do with a grasshopper infestation? It's bad enough we are in the middle of a drought."

Grandfather said, "We will make it through. We always do."

Later that evening, after my mother finished changing the bandages on my leg and arm, she handed me a cup of hot medicine tea. She said, "Drink this. It will help you heal."

Sipping the earthy, aromatic tea of herbs and roots, I decided that tonight I would make a home for my spirit stone.

"Good night," I said to my family.

I closed my room door and lit a kerosene lamp. My room was a "lean-to," a small room built onto the log cabin after my grandparents let us live with them. It was the perfect size for me.

The full moon shone through the window and illuminated my small sculptures crowded together on the windowsill. The log planks above my bed were covered with my drawings and paintings. My art made me happy because it connected me with my old ways.

Quietly I sat and imagined herds of buffalo running free in the tall prairie grass, like a black river disappearing in a point on the horizon. Chiefs lined up, tall and strong, sitting on the backs of the finest horses ever created, with their quillwork decorating them from head to toe, glistening in the sunlight. Collages of majestic designs within prisms of breathtaking color.

Reaching under my bed, I felt around in the darkness until I heard a familiar *ping*. I pulled out the weathered cookie tin used to store some of my personal items and carefully placed it on the bed. The bent tin lid pried off easy enough.

There it was! The round black stone I found over two weeks ago on the bank of the Missouri River. When I picked up the stone, it throbbed in my hand.

I went to work cutting a small circle from a tanned deerskin I used to wrap my eagle feathers. I made holes around the edge of the leather circle with my knife tip and placed the spirit stone and a sprig of sage in the middle of the circle. I finished by lacing the holes closed with a braided deerskin cord.

Good, my spirit stone now had a home, and I now had a medicine bundle. I tied the medicine bundle around my neck and remembered a ceremony I had attended when I was ten.

I'd accompanied my father to a spirit stone healing ceremony. During the ceremony, the lodge filled with blue sparks that lit up the darkness. The sparks flew through the darkness and lit up the room. I could see the bowed and praying heads of the participants. One of the blue lights positioned itself over my head, and I felt it tapping me. I was afraid, and my father told me not to be afraid; the stones were good. He said

Great Spirit used the stones as a vehicle to communicate with us.

The blue sparks were the visible energy created when Great Spirit entered into the stones and talked through them to us. Father said that spirit stones represented eternal truth, because they had no beginning and no end; their power was endless. He reminded me that I could not pick up any stone and declare it a spirit stone.

I was convinced my spirit stone chose me and waited on that path for me for twelve years. I thought about how it warned me about danger. And the golden eagle and the voice of my father that saved me from the wolves. I knew in my gut that my father was alive somewhere and he needed my help. I held my spirit stone and knew the spirits would help me find a way to save our land, and show me where my father was so I could bring him back home.

Burnt Dreams

The dawn hid behind the gray of the eastern sky. It was wild-turkey hunting day! My gun was cleaned and ready; my canvas bag was packed with ammo, a rope, food, water, a hat, a knife, flint, and tobacco for an offering.

The smell of boiling coffee and bacon frying greeted me as I sailed on through the kitchen right toward the outside door. Grandfather said, "Good morning, grandchild."

I answered him from halfway across the front porch. "Good morning, Grandfather."

First order of business was the outhouse. On my walk back toward the house, I stopped and looked up at the visible stars, disappointed that all the thunder and lightning during the night had not brought one raindrop to the parched land.

The kerosene light in the window flooded Orson's silhouette as he walked up the path toward me. We exchanged greetings, and he followed me into the warm kitchen for hot coffee, bacon, and fresh bread.

Grandfather greeted Orson. "Good morning."

Orson greeted him back. "Grandfather, good morning."

Turning to us, Grandfather said, "Eat up, boys. You will need your strength today to bag the legendary grand gobbler."

We both chuckled and hunched over our tin plates, eating like it was our last meal before the big battle. We were anxious to get going toward Medicine Creek to get a jump start on the day. We grabbed our gear by the door and headed out to the barn. Our plan was to ride our horses and tie them up downwind from our blind, or ambush site, which was at the base of the biggest cottonwood tree in Medicine Creek bottom.

Daybreak was still thirty minutes away when we crossed the Iron Nation bluffs and started down the embankment toward Medicine Creek bottom. A herd of antelope ran past us, heading toward the river. In a matter of seconds, all we could see was their white rumps disappearing in the oak brush.

I commented, "That is strange for them to come so close to us."

At that moment, my horse, Anpo, snorted and started sidestepping. Orson's horse, Blake, reared up, almost throwing him to the ground. I

felt my spirit stone burning hot against my chest.
I immediately sensed danger.

I asked Orson, "Can you smell that?"

Orson sniffed the wind like a coyote looking
for dinner. "I do. It smells like smoke," he said.

We both saw it at the same time, a reddish glow
in the southeast horizon that lit up the dark sky.

"Fire!" I shouted.

The wind quickened, and the fire became
brighter with each gust. We were close enough
to hear the roar of the fire. Anpo and Blake were
both terrified and ready to run for cover.

I shouted to Orson, "It looks like it is our
land that is on fire. We need to get help! Now!"
The smell of smoke grew thicker by the minute.
I positioned my rear end above my saddle and
hightailed it toward Iron Nation. We opened up
our horses to a full gallop, and within minutes I
was running across the front porch and through
the front door.

I hollered at the top of my lungs. "Fire!"

Grandfather, Grandmother, and Mother jumped
up from the table. "Where? When? How?"

I pointed toward the southwest. "Over there
toward Medicine Creek! It's our land, Grandfather!"

Grandfather ran his large hands over his ashen
face. He said, "Hoka Hey! Alfred, harness the horses
to the wagon and help me get the plow loaded. I

will take the team on ahead. Orson, you ride into the community and round up whoever you can find. Let them know we have a fire and need their help. Remind them to grab their shovels."

Orson rode out toward Uncle Jay's, and I rushed to the barn to harness the three workhorses and hook them up to the wagon. Grandfather joined me, and we loaded the steel plow onto the wagon. Grandfather climbed up into the wagon seat and turned the horses and wagon southeast toward the fire.

He shouted back to me. "Ride up the hill to Harvey Two Crow. Let him and his sons know we need their help. Quickly! You can catch up with me at Medicine Creek bottom."

I rode full speed toward Harvey's and met him in his yard. He had already been told, and he was ready to go with his three sons. I rode on toward Albert White Bear's and let him know. Although it had taken but a few minutes to gather a large group of men together, it seemed like an eternity.

The group of thundering hooves galloped full speed toward Medicine Creek bottom. When we caught up with Grandfather, a thick blanket of yellow-white smoke covered the prairie sky above Iron Nation. The fire popped and crackled, licking at the dry land, flaring through thickets of dead wood, haystacks, and grassland. Sending wildlife running for cover away from the fire and us.

I could feel the heat on my face. Grandfather had the plow hooked up behind the team of horses and was turning up the earth in a fire line. I helped Grandfather and held the plow handles steady. The plow horses snorted and balked in panic. We fought hard to keep them moving ahead. The plow broke the earth open in a deep single furrow adjacent to the approaching main fire.

The group of men knew what to do, and they leaped into action with shovels, rakes, hoes, and sheer grit, building a firebreak.

Grandfather shouted to Orson, "The horses smell the smoke and are getting spooked. Take them to the end of the pasture, upwind from the fire, and tie them up."

Orson ran with the horses toward a section of a corner cedar post and tied the frightened horses securely, then ran back to help me hold the plow steady.

We worked steadily, back and forth, until we had a good-size fire line. Uncle Jay started a fire on the south side of the furrow nearest the main fire, and a second group of men started a burn line from the other end.

The men worked side by side in a line of flashing shovels and scorching heat. We finished the plowline just as the main fire roared right up against the fire line, trying to lick its way to the other side.

I felt strange. I could not stop staring at the fire. I watched it turn and twist in agony. The fire stared back; two dark gaping holes looked right into my eyes, triggering a memory from long ago.

I had been helping my father tend a sacred fire for a sweat lodge ceremony. I was throwing small sticks into the fire and watching them explode. My father warned me not to play with the fire because it was alive. I thought that notion sounded pretty darn silly, and continued to play with the fire. Without a warning, the fire turned and looked at me, eyes blazing, mouth open, hissing and breathing. The fire shot hot coals into the air, the bigger ones barely missing me but a smaller one hitting me right smack in the forehead. I had a burn blister for days and a red burn scab for many months. I never forgot the day that fire showed me its power. I sure did learn my lesson that day.

Grandfather shouted, "Alfred, what's the matter with you? Move back away from the fire guard! Now!"

I jumped back, shaking the strange feeling off my shoulders.

It looked like the main fire had died down with nowhere to go, finally giving up its life force.

Grandfather moaned in disbelief. "It took us all day, but it is done. We might have a few hot spots we need to keep an eye on, but it looks like the fire is out."

He called the men together and shook each hand in gratitude, many of them his family, his friends, even a couple of strangers. Grandfather looked out across his burned land. He asked the men to form a circle. They did.

Blackened with soot from head to toe, head bowed in humble gratitude, Grandfather prayed: "Thank you, Great Spirit, for the help you sent us today and for keeping every man and animal safe. Thank you for helping us contain this holy and powerful fire. I pray the act of good today will serve to heal the soul of our community and give us all a better day tomorrow. We are all related."

Grandfather told Orson to go get the horses so the men could get back to their homes and families. Grandfather, Uncle Jay, Orson, and I stayed behind.

Uncle Jay walked across the road and squatted down near a clump of tall buffalo grass. He stood up and motioned for us to join him.

Pointing to the ground, he said, "Those tire marks in the damp earth where the artesian spring seeps up to the surface are fresh. The tire tread is unusual, most likely a government vehicle.

Something is not quite right with this picture, and I think we should not give up until we find out."

We all agreed.

Uncle Jay continued walking around the tire tracks like a bobcat circling its prey. He muttered to himself every few steps. "I really need to get a plaster casting of the tire tracks. I think I have a small bag of plaster somewhere in one of my sheds. Hmm, I need to remember where. Hmm."

Grandfather asked, "Jay, do you think Mr. O'Neil had something to do with this fire?"

Uncle Jay stood up. "Yup, I do, Tom. I think Mr. O'Neil sent two of his guys here yesterday to stake out you and your land. They came back out here before dawn and started this fire. Yup, I have no doubt, but proving it will be a challenge because we are up against the big boys."

Tracks Tell Stories

Grandfather leaned against a cedar fence post, looking at the burned land.

He adjusted his straw hat and told us, "When I was at Lower Brule Agency Tribal Office last month, I ran into my old friend Joe Driving Cloud. Joe told me that Mr. O'Neil has been blatantly forcing Tribal members to sell or turn over their allotted lands back to the Tribe for little or nothing. Joe said Mr. O'Neil, the Lower Brule Sioux chairperson; Mitch Schnapp, a local banker; and several high officials in the Office of Indian Affairs are involved in an illegal operation.

"They are tampering with land documents and forcing Tribal members out of their allotments. They are taking the newly acquired lands and subleasing them out to white ranchers for large amounts of money. Ever since my conversation with Joe Driving Cloud, I was afraid this might happen to us. Our land is prime river bottom and close to a good water source."

Uncle Jay shook his head. "It is a sad day for us when the Office of Indian Affairs puts a white man in charge to govern our affairs, and this white man is our worst enemy. He does not respect our culture and is as crooked as a dog's leg."

Uncle Jay continued. "Mother Nature has eyes everywhere. Someone or something will eventually reveal the truth."

I said, "We must not let word get back to Superintendent O'Neil that we know he is responsible for starting this fire. He is dangerous and desperate."

Uncle Jay pointed to the ground. "Most important, we must play along and be patient and continue to collect hard evidence, like these tire tracks here."

Grandfather chimed in. "When we get enough evidence, we will present it to officials above Superintendent O'Neil's head, with hopes of getting him charged and removed."

We all nodded in agreement.

Uncle Jay said, "I think it is important to get a casting of those tire tracks before they disappear." He turned to Orson and me. "Do you boys mind staying here for a while longer? I want to ride home and get a bag of plaster I have left over from when I replastered our kitchen. It will take me an

hour to ride home and get back here. Besides, I
want you to keep an eye out for any hot spots that
flare up until I get back."

"Sure, we can stay here," we both answered.
"It is not a problem."

I helped Grandfather lift the steel plow back
onto the wagon, and he climbed up into the seat
and turned the tired team toward home.

After Grandfather and Uncle Jay left, Orson
and I walked toward the grassy creek bank where
we had Anpo and Blake tied up. Anpo greeted
me with his high-pitched whinny, and I am sure
in horse language it was a dandy scolding for
leaving him tied up for so long.

I said, "You were safe here with plenty of
grass and water."

We walked back to guard the tire tracks and
wait for Uncle Jay. We were both thirsty and
hungry and sat on the ground, drinking water
from our canvas canteen and eating pemmican
we had brought for the turkey hunt. Orson wanted
to know all the details regarding Superintendent
O'Neil, so I filled him in on every last one.

I told Orson how Superintendent O'Neil
visited my grandparents' home two weeks ago
unannounced, that he blatantly told my grandfather
he wanted our land, and that Grandfather told him
he was not interested in selling. "Superintendent

O'Neil said he would get the land one way or another. Now this. I think Superintendent O'Neil means to harm us all," I said.

Orson shook his head in disbelief. "Alfred, you are my best friend. Your family has always treated me like their own blood. I will help you stop this man any way I can. But we must plan it carefully and not let anyone know our plans until we are ready to act. I know our friend Billy White Plume and a few others will help us. We cannot wait too long like your uncle Jay and your grandfather want. We must act quickly; Superintendent O'Neil must be stopped before he incites more violence and hurts other families."

I told Orson, "We will get Billy White Plume and a few other friends together to work out a plan to save our land and reveal Superintendent O'Neil for the crook he is."

Just as I was going to tell Orson about my spirit stone, Uncle Jay rode up with a gunny sack, a bag of plaster, a can, a canvas bag of water, and two wooden sticks. He motioned to us. "Okay, boys, help me get unloaded, and let's get started."

I mixed the plaster in the can with a wooden stick while Orson slowly poured water into the can. We finished mixing. Uncle Jay seemed satisfied with the consistency, so we poured the liquid plaster slurry into the tire tracks until we had a good fill.

Uncle Jay told us, "Thank you both. You boys go home. There is nothing more you can do here. I am going to stay behind until the plaster cast cures and watch for hot spots that might flare up."

We thanked Uncle Jay for staying behind, and Orson and I rode home with the last rays of sunlight falling fast.

As we started for home, I thought, *I wish I had told Orson about my spirit stone today, but it was not the right time.* Instead I said, "Let's not get discouraged, friend. Let us plan to go turkey hunting again in the morning."

Orson agreed, smiling at me with his tired eyes. "I will see you early tomorrow, my friend." We shook hands, and he turned and headed down the road toward his home.

I unsaddled Anpo. After giving him feed and water, I brushed him down, telling him what a great friend he was to me. I knew with our hay and feed burned to the ground, Anpo and the rest of the livestock would be facing some lean days ahead. I let Anpo out in the pasture and shuffled toward the back porch to wash up.

Mother heard the creaking wood planks under my heavy feet and opened the door. It was dark by now, and she carried a kerosene lamp out to me.

She said, "Son, when you are finished, come in to eat. I kept your supper warm for you." My mother was a good Lakota mother. She fanned me with cedar smoke and sage to clean the negative residue from my shoulders.

I nibbled at her biscuits and potato soup. Out of the corner of my eye, I watched Grandfather sitting quietly on the other side of the stove.

When I finished, I went and sat down beside him and told him, "Grandfather, you are my protector and my teacher. I love you deeply and honor you greatly. I will work hard and help you all I can. I hope you have a good night."

Grandfather nodded in affirmation, but I could see the worry in his silent, tired eyes.

Chepa curled up below my bed, and I crawled under the safety of my buffalo robe and looked out the window at many stars sprinkled across the night sky. My mind drifted toward the land of dreams. Despite all the broken treaties, the land grabs, and the physical destruction meant to wipe my people off the face of the earth, we were still here. Because of the prayers from our ancestors— like Chief Iron Nation, Chief Sitting Bull, Chief Red Cloud, and many other grandmothers and grandfathers—we survived, and we would always survive. Someday in the future, we would be as many as those stars above.

Rattlesnake Hideout

Orson showed up extra early, anxious to get going on our turkey hunt. After a hot bowl of cornmeal mush, we were ready to go. Grandfather fanned us with cedar smoke for protection. I put Chepa inside the barn. Mother would let him out when she gathered eggs later. We saddled our horses, Anpo and Blake, and at last we were on our way to hunt turkey.

We noticed numerous turkey tracks in the mud at the edge of the timberline along Medicine Creek. It didn't take us long to gather enough dead and downed ash to build a well-hidden blind at the base of the biggest cottonwood tree in the region.

We walked our horses downwind and tied them up, with plenty of grass and water. We walked back and settled into our blind, listening for the sound of gobbles, gurgles, yelps, or clucks alerting us to nearby wild turkeys. The only sound was the cooing of a few mourning doves and the screech of a red-tailed hawk circling overhead, scouting for a rodent or two.

Orson was the first to hear the loud gobbles off in the distance. I spotted the flock of turkeys up the gully to the right, bathed in the golden light reaching through the dense woods. They were heading our way.

I sprinkled my offering of tobacco on the ground, a prayer of gratitude for the life that would be taken to feed our hungry families and extend our lives. I rested my barrel on a rock and waited patiently. I sat still, sweating with nervous hope.

In a matter of minutes, the flock was in front of our blind, and the old lead gobbler strutted out in front, protecting his flock. Although we were well hidden, he immediately sensed our presence and lifted his tail feathers in confrontation. The fleshy growth around his bald head turned bright red, white, and blue, and he was ready for a fight.

Close behind him, two juvenile jake gobblers stepped forward and strutted toward us. I took it as a sign they would be the ones to sacrifice their lives today and to let the old gobbler continue to lead his flock.

I whispered to Orson, "I will go for the young jake to the left, and you aim for the one to the right."

Orson nodded in agreement. I held my breath and aimed. I pulled the trigger, and Orson pulled his a second later. Two shots ricocheted through the corridor of the wooded creek, and both turkeys fell to the ground.

The intruding noise set the creek bottom alive with a flurry of activity. The skies above us turned dark with field sparrows rousted from the treetops, scattering in a chorus of high, thin whistles: "Zeeee-zee-zee." The flock, gobbling deep-throated "kee-kees," made their run toward the safety of the thickets, followed by numerous rabbits scurrying away from us.

It was midmorning, and we had our catch. We dressed the birds out and carried them to our horses. We packed them over our shoulders and headed for home. I took the lead through the tall grass, avoiding hidden badger holes.

We reached a rocky embankment, and Anpo started balking and did not want to go any farther. I pulled on his reins and coaxed him up the embankment. Too late. He reared up, and I fell onto the rocks.

I kept falling and plunged downward into a huge hole on the southeast side of the rocky embankment. The wind was knocked right out of me. The first thing I noticed in the dim light was bare ground with large clumps of dirt all around me. An eerie silence filled the space, and a terrible stench stung my nostrils.

In a few seconds, the air was filled with the deafening whir of hundreds of hard rattles, clacking from side to side. The dirt clumps started moving, and I recognized the flat triangular heads, tongues flicking to detect an enemy.

The clumps around me were blades of grass with rattlesnakes curled tightly in balls around each one. I had fallen into a rattlesnake den, and I had disturbed their slumber. I had no idea what I was in store for, but it couldn't be good. I could feel my heart pounding in my head, and I was covered with goose bumps.

My spirit stone inside the medicine bundle around my neck burned hot against my chest. I knew I was in extreme danger, and I had to get out of there fast. I did not dare make another noise, but the rattlesnakes sensed my body heat and crawled toward me.

I could hear Orson calling down to me. "Alfred, what happened? Are you all right?"

I moved quickly. Jumping up, I climbed toward the light above. I grabbed Orson's extended hand. He pulled me through the earthen opening.

I could not find my voice, but I croaked out, "Rattlesnakes! Run!" Every size imaginable was crawling out of the den to catch the morning sun rays. We scrambled down the hillside toward the horses. They were both grazing far away from the den.

Orson asked, "Are you hurting? Did you get bit?"

I answered, "Yes, I hurt everywhere. I am sure I have a hundred rattlesnake bites all over my body."

Orson helped me hobble to the safety of the open field near the horses. I was profusely sweating, and I could feel that my face was flushed and hot. I removed my clothing, and the bitter chill of the morning slapped life into my bare skin.

Orson carefully inspected every inch of my skin for small puncture holes. After a few minutes, he said, "Alfred, I cannot find one snakebite. You are okay. I think it was too cold for the snakes to move fast enough to strike you."

I was not convinced, and I had him do a body check a second time. Again, he said, "Alfred, I see no evidence of a snakebite. Because of the cold temperature, I believe you beat fate and survived this catastrophe unscathed."

I dressed and jumped around to get warmth back into my cold limbs and chattering teeth.

I said, "I should have paid attention to Anpo. He knew something was wrong and smelled the snake den."

Orson agreed. Minutes later, I was still unhinged about my narrow escape. I was sure Grandfather would scold me for not paying attention.

Grandfather had taught me: "Alfred, always pay attention to your horse. It will show you if water and food is safe to eat or if danger is near. Remember, grandchild, your horse could save your life."

Now I knew what he was talking about.

Orson laughed. "What a high price to pay for turkey meat. First a fire and now a rattlesnake den. We got our turkeys, and you survived hundreds of rattlesnakes without a single bite. I would say we had a very successful hunting trip."

As we rode home, I decided to tell Orson about my spirit stone. He listened intently as I shared my fears, my dreams, and my vows to find a way to save our land from Superintendent O'Neil and to find my father. I finished, and we rode in silence for a minute.

Orson said, "I believe I have a solution."

As he told me his solution, I was stunned that I had not seen it before now. The solution was as clear as the bell ringing from the steeple at the Messiah Episcopal Church.

As Good a Time as Any

The ride along the river bottom cradled us in silence. Still a little shaky, I was trying to shake off my close encounter with the snake nation. I tried focusing on the white-tipped cumulonimbus clouds that hung low in the afternoon sky. Thank goodness they provided us occasional shade from the intense sun.

Our horses' hooves swirled the dry dust right through my bandana that I had tied tightly over my nose and mouth. I pulled my bandana down and shouted to Orson over the wailing wind that was getting more intense by the minute: "We should let Anpo and Blake rest and drink water. It will also give us a chance to brush the dirt off our clothes. What do you think?"

Orson gave me a thumbs-up, steering his horse off the road toward the river.

We found a water inlet near a grove of cottonwood trees. The horses didn't need any nudging; they quickly lapped up river water between snorts. Orson and I found a good grassy shaded area and sat down.

After we brushed the road dirt off, Orson cleared his throat like he always did when he was going to say something important. "Friend, I think I know why the stone people chose you to carry a message for them."

I thought, *Maybe this is as good a time as any to have this discussion.* I nodded for him to continue.

Orson said, "It seems there is something greater taking place than the thoughts and images you dream. I remember my grandfather telling me that the physical world is but a counterpart of the spiritual realm. Alfred, I believe your dreamtime is connecting your spirit to that sacred realm where our people live when they leave this world. I see you are deeply searching for answers yet unknown."

I said, "Friend, I know you have the gift to know things and see into the future. I believe you because I know you would not lie to me.

"Yes, I am searching for answers," I continued. "Like, why did my father leave me? Why can I not make sense of my dreams or remember what the spirits are telling me? How can I help my grandfather stand up to O'Neil and his bad men?"

I followed Orson's gaze upward to the swaying treetops and a nest of squirrels chattering and climbing from limb to limb.

After a brief silence, Orson said, "One of the last things my grandfather did for me before he passed was to put me out alone, on the high hilltop behind our home, to cry for a vision. My grandfather told me that everything I needed or wanted to know was not outside of me but deep inside; it was my inner voice. He told me I must fast on a hill and ask the Great Spirit to show me how to be true to myself and how to learn to quiet my mind and recognize the voice. This would be my strength and the foundation that would guide me through life and help me be the best person I can be."

Orson continued. "Alfred, I believe what my grandfather taught me applies to you as well. I believe Great Spirit has sent you a spirit helper in the form of a stone to show you how to listen, believe in yourself, and respect the ancient knowledge. You have a big heart, and you carry the knowledge. Friend, the entire world fits into your heart: people, animals, nature, life, and even death. For many reasons, you are troubled and fearful. Your heart and head are miles apart.

"I believe you need to offer tobacco to Pete Flying Crow and ask him to conduct a crying for a vision ceremony to help you connect your heart and head. You will soon know what to do to help your grandfather save your land and protect your family from O'Neil."

Orson's words made me feel strange, like I was flying through the air in an unfamiliar place and time, but I did not move an inch as I sat and intensely listened to his every word.

Orson lifted his rawhide canteen and gulped water down. We sat a few more minutes in silence and listened to the waves in the distance breaking the surface of the Missouri River, lapping against her shoreline in bursts of white, dusty foam. A colony of Franklin prairie gulls swooped above us, flashing their small black heads and black-and-red bills at us in attempts to protect their nests. "Yeow . . . yeow . . . yeow."

I swept my gaze along the north side of the riverbank, and my eyes stopped on the spot that my grandfather, Elmer, and I welcomed in the new year not too long ago. My hand lightly brushed my spirit stone, tucked safely around my neck, which came to me at that time. Although it was a short time ago, it felt like months had passed.

I said, "Thank you, friend, your words resonate truth and peace. I will prepare to go to Grandfather Pete Flying Crow and ask for help. Now we must get home before this storm overtakes us."

Fierce gusts of wind tore at our hats as we let our horses go into a full gallop and made our way home. Loud claps of thunder followed dancing streaks of pinkish-blue lightning across the western sky. Orson's head was tucked low, and the two hard-earned gobbler feathers whipped from Blake's black mane. When we reached the fork in the road to his house, Orson steered his horse in the right direction and yelled, as his voice trailed away, "See you at school tomorrow . . . Big Heart Boy."

Sparse but heavy raindrops hit my face as I raced toward home. I was grateful I'd made it through the rattlesnake pit in one piece, and I was grateful for Orson's words. I had a lot to share with my grandfather. I decided to tell Grandfather everything about my dreams from start to finish. I just needed to find the right moment.

It was near suppertime; the last rays of daylight peeped through the tall, majestic storm clouds, sending a rainbow across the valley below. I was sure it was just for me: a promise of something wonderful coming my way.

That promise came true the next day when Sage Big Eagle started school at Iron Nation Day School. It was midmorning during our math lessons when the school door opened, and a woman wearing a red wool blanket coat and curled bobbed hair came in. At first, I thought she was alone, until she reached behind her back and nudged a girl of thirteen out toward the front of the classroom.

The new girl was the prettiest girl I had ever seen. She had the longest, blackest hair. Most striking were her deep blue eyes, just like a clear sky on a summer's day. You could have heard a pin drop. She looked like she was about to faint from fright. The muffled giggles from the back of the classroom sure didn't help matters.

The woman in the red coat looked a lot like Mrs. Red Elk. She whispered a few things to our teacher and stepped back through the door, leaving the young girl alone and shaking. Mrs. Red Feather had us clear an area for her. I went to the shed behind the schoolhouse and pulled a desk from storage. I wiped away as much dust as I could and carried it in.

Of course, I placed it next to my desk. I figured I would be the welcoming party before Orson stepped in. I flashed her my best smile, and she gave me a timid half smile back.

That afternoon on my way home, I felt elated and full of energy. Elmer gave me strange side-glances, noticing my giddy behavior. I wanted to skip all the way home, but as we came near the house, a thick brown dust swirled in the air.

My joy quickly turned to desolation when I saw the familiar black Model T Ford parked by the front gate. The door opened, and a pair of brown shiny shoes stepped into view. Elmer and I both let out a strained sigh.

Elmer said, "Oh no! It's Superintendent O'Neil. I wonder what he's up to now."

Unfortunately, I knew.

Papers in the Wind

uperintendent O'Neil was carrying a stack of papers, tied together with a faded string, as he stomped toward the house. Elmer and I met him when he was halfway to the porch. We knew by the way he held the papers tight against his chest that they must be important.

He said, "Ohhh, what a trip. Young fellas, is your grandfather, Thomas Plenty Buffalo, home?"

I answered him, ignoring Chepa's deep menacing growls coming from his secret ambush hole under the front porch. "I will check inside and let you know."

I stuck my head in the doorway. "Grandfather, are you here? Superintendent O'Neil is here to see you."

Grandfather stepped through the door and into the light. With squinting eyes, he said, "How can I help you?"

Superintendent O'Neil made the first move to close the distance between himself and the front porch. He extended his hand toward Grandfather, but Grandfather ignored the gesture.

Grandfather said, "If you are here for more land talk, I told you our land is not for sale! I am not planning to change my mind anytime soon. I recommend you leave and not come back again."

Light crimson spots slowly crept up Superintendent O'Neil's neck and face. He lifted his soft, delicate hands and shook a finger at us. "I have tried very hard to be nice, but things are about to change. Mark my words, Mr. Plenty Buffalo, you and your family will regret this moment!"

At that moment, Chepa came dashing out from under the porch like an erupting volcano, a flurry of barks and growls, aiming straight for Superintendent O'Neil. The superintendent made a beeline—in his slick, shiny shoes—down the path toward the safety of his shiny government Model T.

He'd almost made it when he tripped on a stone and his legs shot out from under his massive body. He went airborne, and when he landed in the grass, he desperately tried to hold on to his bundle of papers. The next moment, it was as if a hand reached down from the heavens and pulled the tattered end of the frayed, worn string.

In a split second, a dozen parchment papers were set free to dance in the Dakota wind. Superintendent O'Neil went up on all fours and clawed at the empty air around him, trying desperately to catch the runaway papers. He appeared more concerned with the papers than his own well-being.

We all stood paralyzed by the unexpected display before us. Even Chepa turned his head from side to side, watching in astonishment.

Without a glance in our direction, Superintendent O'Neil, his face as red as a beet, pried the papers from the thorny, dry thistles. He stomped to his Model T and secured the papers in the seat next to him.

Before we knew it, he headed down the road, leaving us all in a cloud of dust.

Grandfather started shaking like a bowl of pudding. A deep belly laugh filled the porch. Soon we were all in stitches, except Grandmother.

"Oh my goodness, what a sight," Grandmother said, trying to stay composed, but she soon joined us in a good laugh at the trickster's folly with Superintendent O'Neil.

Grandfather brushed the tears from his laughing eyes. He herded us toward the barnyard and said, "Okay, boys, chore time—I mean manure time. Grandchild Alfred, you can shovel the manure from the stalls. Grandchild Elmer, you can clean the chicken coop out and gather the eggs."

Elmer walked toward the chicken coop but then stopped in his tracks. He pointed toward the barbwire fence. "Look, Alfred, are those some of Superintendent O'Neil's papers?"

I looked in the direction where Elmer was pointing. Several papers were caught on the dirt drifts along the fence line. I couldn't believe my eyes. Some of O'Neil's papers! I gathered all of them up; a few were stapled together. The papers were letters, and all of them had signatures signed in ink. The letters were from the Office of Indian Affairs in Washington, DC. I couldn't believe what I was reading.

March 23, 1929

Department of the Interior
Office of Indian Affairs
Washington, DC 20515

Mr. James O'Neil
Supt. Lower Brule Agency

Dear Mr. O'Neil:

It has been brought to my attention that the land transaction between Mr. Thomas Plenty Buffalo, a Lower Brule Sioux, and the Indian

Office has not been signed by Mr. Plenty Buffalo. It appears Mr. Plenty Buffalo's land moved out of allotment status some years ago, and he owns a free and clear title. It also appears that Mr. Plenty Buffalo has been using his land for agricultural purposes, and he is up to date on all required taxes. We assume Mr. Plenty Buffalo understands moving his clear-titled land into surplus-land status will allow settlers and other parties to take possession of such land. Therefore, in order to file a legal document, we need Mr. Plenty Buffalo to sign the attached paper, notarize it, and return it to our office, Department of the Interior, as soon as possible.

Ray L. Wilbur
Secretary of the Interior

Along with the three signed letters that were stapled together were three other unsigned documents. I sat down on a nearby rock, stunned by what I was holding and how the wind spirits had placed them in my care.

I now understood that Superintendent O'Neil's plan was to force my grandfather into signing the land transaction. Now, without the original letters from the Office of Indian Affairs, he would not be able to put his plan into place. I thought,

I must hide the papers immediately, because once Superintendent O'Neil realizes they are missing, he will come back with full vengeance.

I quietly slipped past Grandmother, who was working in her garden, and into the house. In my room, I placed the valuable letters inside my school bag and slid the bag under my bed until I could hide them in a better place.

Elmer was waiting for me with a confused look on his round, innocent face. I said, "Little brother, please don't tell Grandfather what we found. It is very dangerous right now. I will tell him later."

Elmer, his big brown eyes wide with wonder, said, "Okay, Alfred. I won't say one word. I promise."

I trusted that my secret was safe with my little brother, but I knew I had to tell Orson what had happened. He would know what to do.

Even though the threats from Superintendent O'Neil loomed over my family, I still felt different tonight. I felt an excitement, and I could not wait to get to school tomorrow. As I slowly drifted off, my sleepy eyes flew open with a fearful thought: *What if Sage likes Orson instead of me? I must tell Orson that Sage Big Eagle is hands-off. She saw me first, and I cannot explain it, but I know she likes me too.* My plan was comforting. I smiled my way to sleep . . . grateful for such a wonderful day.

The next day I cornered Orson during morning recess and came right to the point. "Hey, Orson, what do you think of the new girl, Sage Big Eagle?"

He said, "She's okay. What do you think, Alfred?"

I answered, "I think she is the prettiest girl I have ever seen."

Orson knew me well. He watched my hands fidget inside my pockets.

He said, "What's on your mind, my friend?"

I rallied up my courage. "Orson, please don't flirt with Sage like you do with all the new girls. Give me a chance, because I really like her a lot."

Orson threw his head back and let out a bellow. "Well . . . well, I think you have finally been stung by the love bug. Don't worry about me. I think she is already smitten with you . . ." He winked at me. "I am sure she will probably run for the hills when she finds out how stubborn you are . . . Ha ha."

I didn't laugh because I did not think that was very funny, even though he was trying to lighten up my serious tone. It felt good to get my point across to my best friend, Orson.

Most of all, it felt good to know I would not have to compete for Sage's attention.

Life was good. Or was it?

Heart and Bones

T he following week passed in a blur. I spent every minute I could at school to be near Sage. On my way home from school, I had to watch out, because the possibility of danger from Superintendent O'Neil and his men was real.

Grandfather was doing all he could do to protect us. He slept during the day so he could be on watch all night. He started keeping his rifle close by. I could see that stress was taking a toll on him. When we heard gunshots two weeks ago, I tried to go with Grandfather to investigate. He told me to stay inside and that he would handle everything.

The next morning, Grandfather had a black eye and a swollen lip, but he wouldn't tell me what had happened. I knew things were really tough when Grandfather asked Harvey Two Crow and his boys to help us round up some livestock. He sold fifty head of cattle and nine horses at the Fort Pierre sale because we did not have enough feed. To make things worse, the drought was drying everything up, and the grasshoppers were slowly arriving.

Every night I asked the spirits for a dream to show me what to do. Every morning all I could remember were images of a giant sky spirit lifting me up into the heavens. As I was being lifted, I couldn't escape, and I was sucked into a deep, dark abyss of unknowns and fearful feelings.

Things took a turn on Friday. It was the last day of our school year, which meant a whole lot of horsing around and special snacks many of us students brought from home to share.

The day started out good, but then someone wrote a love note to Sage, on my slate, and hung it on the front of Mrs. Red Feather's desk. I knew it was Junior White Hail's sloppy printing. It was all I needed, for Junior to show off and try to fight me in front of Sage.

I felt a sensation like hot honey creep up my neck toward my ears. I knew by the glances from the other students that my discomfort was obvious.

At the end of the day, everyone cleaned desks, washed the blackboard, swept the floor, and stacked our slates in the tall cabinet in the back corner. Sage and I packed up a crate of special books for Mrs. Red Elk and carried them out to her Chrysler Fargo truck with the peeling paint.

As we walked, I said, "Sage . . . um . . . I'm sorry about what happened today with the message. Junior likes to cause me trouble."

She shrugged. "That's okay. I am not worried about it."

I walked slow, but we reached the truck too soon.

"Um . . . ," I said as I worked up my courage to say, "I am also sorry that you just started school and now the school year is over."

Sage said, "I wish I would have moved here sooner. Since my family is moving to Denver, my mother thought it would be best if I stayed with my aunt for the summer and maybe even next year too."

What great news!

All of a sudden, I said, "Sage, do you want to come with me to the community field tomorrow?"

Sage said, "Why?"

I explained. "Every third Saturday afternoon in the summer, we have a stickball game at the community field. Me, Orson, and a whole bunch of kids from Cedar Creek and Lower Brule. We all get together and play against one another. It is really fun . . . Even though we lose a lot, it is still fun."

She smiled a wide white smile at me. "Sure, Alfred, I would love that. I will ask my aunt if it's okay. If she agrees, I will see you tomorrow."

The next morning passed in a blur of chores and anticipation. Finally, I made it to the community field. When I saw Orson sitting on the field, I threw my shoes down and sat next to him.

He said, "What's up, Alfred?"

I decided the time had come to confide in someone about the hidden papers and O'Neil's devious plan.

"A whole lot," I answered.

I didn't waste a minute and went straight to the point. I told Orson about the superintendent's visit and finding the letters. While I told him everything, Orson let out a few hoots and slapped his knee.

I said, "Orson, what should I do? I am afraid for my grandfather. What if Superintendent O'Neil harms him because he thinks he has the letters?"

Orson said, "I have your back, Alfred. I believe your spirit helper placed the letters in your path and is showing you a solution. Remember our talk, Alfred. You need to look inside for the answers."

I nodded my understanding just as team players started showing up. In a few minutes, Mrs. Red Elk's truck pulled up, and Sage jumped out.

"Hi, Sage. I'm glad you could join us today," I called out.

We joined the others to designate our teams and go over the rules.

Before I knew it, the shadows were long, and the teams were on their way home. Our Iron Nation team won for the first time in a long time. I felt glad that Sage could play with us, and she was really good.

I waved goodbye to Sage and said, "I hope I see you next week, and thanks for coming. It was fun."

She nodded, smiling in agreement. "See you later, Alfred. Thanks for inviting me."

Orson and I walked over and sat on one of the wooden benches used for spectators.

"Orson," I said, "I have a plan. This morning I put the land papers I hid in my cookie tin inside the hollow of the big cottonwood tree down by the dried-up pond where we used to fish. I know they will be safe there. Next, I want to form a group to help. You, me, Sage, Elizabeth, and maybe a few other friends, like the Yellow Hat Twins, Todd and Tim. What do you think?"

Orson thought for a moment and said, "I think it's a good start. We can meet on Monday and maybe follow up next weekend. Elizabeth's aunt works at the agency at Lower Brule across from Superintendent O'Neil, and I am sure she can help us too."

We shook hands and called it a deal, and then we both headed home in different directions.

My head was full of plans and my heart full of emotions, so I did not notice a Model T pulling up next to me. Before I knew it, I was punched in the jaw and fell facedown in the dirt. A worn boot was heavy on my neck, so I couldn't see who was standing above me. I did recognize the voices of Superintendent O'Neil and his men, Big Jim and Jess Miller.

One of the men said, "Where are the papers, son? We don't want to hurt you; we just want the land papers. You tell us where the papers are, and we will leave you and your grandfather alone."

I managed to spit a mouthful of dirt out. "I don't have the papers. Even if I did, I sure wouldn't give them to you."

That sent the boot deeper into my neck.

The other man said, "You can count on us coming back until we find those papers. Oh, by the way, tell your grandfather to pay attention to those shadows around his property. They carry guns."

The foot lifted off my neck, and while I lay on the ground, I watched black shiny shoes and worn-down boots climb into the vehicle. They sped off, leaving a cloud of dust behind them.

I sat up and looked around. I was definitely alone. I brushed myself off, thinking how glad I was that Elmer wasn't with me today. I would hate to see my brother hurt. By the time I made it home, I had quite a headache. Grandfather was standing at the front gate waiting for me. I knew immediately something was wrong. I was shocked to see my grandfather's bruised eye and busted lip. He was just as shocked looking back at me.

Grandfather said, "Are you okay, grandson?"

"Yes, Grandfather, I am," I answered. "It was Superintendent O'Neil, Big Jim, and Jess Miller."

"This is getting out of hand when they force their way into our home and turn everything upside down," Grandfather said. "They didn't hurt your grandmother, but she was very scared. Elmer was with your mother at Leda's. They jumped me just as I rode in and said they wanted the land papers. I told them I didn't know what they were talking about, but they didn't believe me. They finally left and said they would be back. We must make protection prayers and let our family and friends know what is happening to us."

I felt responsible for everything. *Maybe I should just turn the land papers over to Superintendent O'Neil and trust that he will leave us alone.* But deep down I knew that was not the answer. I was torn and did not know what to do.

My grandmother gasped when I entered the house and she saw the blood on my face and my swollen lip. She quickly heated water to clean my face. She was talking under her breath in Lakota, talking so fast I couldn't understand a word.

Later, when I was in bed, my mother and Elmer arrived. I could hear the muffled voices of Grandfather and Grandmother in the kitchen giving a recap of the afternoon events to my mother.

Just as I drifted off to sleep, a vision of my great-aunt Pearl, Grandmother's eldest sister, came to me. She lived two miles northwest of us. I reached for my black stone, and as it grew warm in my hand, I knew I had to pay her a visit and tell her what was happening to our land.

Out in the yard, Chepa's barks told us we were being watched. I prayed my family and our animals would be safe tonight, but I especially prayed for my grandfather as he watched over us. All alone.

Two of a Kind

I t was a beautiful Saturday morning with the sun still low in the eastern sky and dew glistening everywhere. After I finished breakfast and did all my chores, I told my mother I was going to visit my great-aunt Pearl—or just Aunt Pearl, as I called her. My mother was worried and didn't want me to travel alone, but I told her it was very important that I talk to Aunt Pearl.

My mother said okay but reminded me to watch out for O'Neil's men.

I saddled Anpo and used a piece of rawhide to tightly tie the canvas school bag with the land papers onto the back of my saddle. I tied my long rifle to the side of the saddle. Anpo, Chepa, and I then started down the three-mile stretch along the river toward Aunt Pearl's.

Mother and I waved goodbye to each other.

Anpo's rhythmic stride made it easy for my mind to wander . . . I remembered Grandmother telling me that her sister Pearl had been a teacher at Haskell United States Indian Industrial Training School in Kansas for many years. Five years ago she moved back to Iron Nation with her husband, Ray Hand. He passed away last year, and she now lived alone in her log cabin near the ruins of an old abandoned US Army post. I liked to check in on her, and she always had a knack of making a whole lot of sense to me.

I had to knock a few times on Aunt Pearl's door before she opened up.

She looked puzzled until she recognized me. "Oh my goodness, what a pleasant surprise. Come in, grandchild. How are you? How is your mother? Grandchild Elmer? What about my sister Lucille and brother-in-law Thomas? Oh my, excuse me . . . please come in."

"It is good to see you, Auntie," I said. "My mother, brother Elmer, grandmother, and grandfather are all well. They send their best wishes and prayers."

I gave her my best big bear hug and followed her inside.

The atmosphere inside her home was always comforting. Sunlight spilled across the wooden kitchen floor from four large windows on the southeast side of her cabin. House plants and dwarf tomato vines lined the south side of her room. The air smelled of sweetgrass, sage, and dried herbs. A typewriter sat on her kitchen table next to a stack of papers and a Montgomery Ward & Co. catalog.

She straightened her long thin white braids against her dark blue trade-cloth dress with the sewn-on elk teeth and said, "Excuse the mess. I was working on a letter on behalf of a dear friend of mine, Ben Reifel. He is attending South Dakota State College and is paying for his own tuition. I am writing letters to my friends to help me find a foundation that might be able to help him with his education."

She motioned for me to sit down on the bench next to her kitchen table while she made us mint tea.

She went on to explain, "Ben is interested in running for a South Dakota state government office when he finishes school. He even talked about organizing a 'New Deal' to end cultural assimilation and the allotment of our lands."

Her words caught my attention and caused my thoughts to race: *This is why my inner voice told me to come here today . . . I need to tell Mother and definitely Grandmother and Grandfather about Ben Reifel. I am sure he can help us save our land.*

After we comfortably settled in, Aunt Pearl got straight to the point. "Grandson Alfred, you look worried today. Tell me, what is on your mind?"

I pulled the land papers out of the bag and started telling her the tale from the beginning. I told her everything that had happened regarding Superintendent O'Neil. She listened intently. The more I talked, the more Aunt Pearl pursed her lips together. While she looked through the papers, her pretty brown and wrinkled face was set in determination.

When I finished telling her everything, she looked me right in the eyes and said, "I will get Benjamin Reifel to help and whoever else I can to help. You do not need to worry your young mind about these matters."

Aunt Pearl put more water in the teakettle as I stoked her cookstove with wood. In no time the bright flames caught, and the kettle was heating water for more tea. She dug around in her cupboard and found a plate of her famous sugar cookies.

Setting the cookies down in front of me, she said, "Help yourself, grandson."

When I finished eating, Aunt Pearl looked at the wind-up clock on the wall and said, "I sure enjoyed your visit, grandchild Alfred. The sun is still high in the sky, and it is time for you to get home. My sister and brother-in-law will start to worry soon."

I woke Chepa, who had been sleeping on the porch in the sunlight next to his old friend Whiskers, Aunt Pearl's cat.

"Tell your grandparents I will have Ben Reifel look into a few land issues involving Superintendent O'Neil, and I will get back to all of you soon." Aunt Pearl waved at me for a long time as I set off toward home.

I waved back and headed along the river bottom road. A mile into our ride, Chepa started barking at a stray dog. The dog was a German shepherd with a clipped right ear. The dog seemed distressed and kept running back toward the riverbank.

I recognized the dog. It belonged to that bully, Junior White Hail. My first impulse was to run, but something in my heart told me to stay and find out what was going on. I followed the German shepherd down the bank to a dark green inlet.

I could see the head of Junior White Hail bobbing in the water. He was in a whirlpool that was sucking him into the river's current. I didn't hesitate. I found a long piece of driftwood and placed it close enough for him to grab, but he couldn't reach it. He was exhausted from fighting the whirlpool, and he went under.

When his head disappeared, I peeled my jacket off and dived in. I felt his head and grabbed him by the hair. I held on to him and swam in the current until I found a shallow sandbar that reached to the shore as it broke the force of the water.

I pulled Junior up onto the shore and immediately pushed on his chest to get the excess water out of his lungs. Within a few minutes, he spurted, and water shot from his mouth. He sat up, coughing and gagging. When he was able to take some deep breaths, he couldn't believe his eyes that it was me who saved him.

"Thank you, Alfred. I thought I was a goner," he said.

I said, "No problem. Your dog is the one to thank. He found us and led us to you."

Junior called his dog. "Jaber Boy! Come here, boy."

His dog Jaber ran to him and licked his face.

I didn't see Junior's horse, so I asked Junior if he wanted a ride home. He was silent for a bit but finally said, "Sure, I have a headache, and I feel weak."

I whistled, and within a few minutes, Anpo came to me. I climbed up onto the saddle and pulled Junior behind me.

On the way home, I asked, "Why were you out in the river alone?"

Junior answered, "My father passed away last year, and I have been very sad because I miss him a lot. We used to come to this spot and fish. Today I missed him more than usual, so I wanted to visit here. I got too close to the river, and I fell in by accident."

Now I understood why Junior was angry at most everyone, especially me. Perhaps he picked on me because I was just like him, fatherless.

"Alfred," Junior said, "I am really sorry for how I have been acting toward you. I really wanted to ask you to be my friend, but I was afraid you would say no because you already had Orson for a friend."

I turned halfway in my saddle and reached my hand back to shake his hand. "I would be happy to be your friend."

We followed the road that took us to the cabin where Junior lived. A little white-haired woman stood on the front porch. When Junior slid off my horse, she saw the shape Junior was in.

"Grandson, where were you? I was worried," she said. "Are you okay? You are all wet."

I introduced myself as Lucille and Thomas Plenty Buffalo's grandson and told her what had happened at the river. She looked at Junior with sadness in her eyes.

"I need to get home while I still have daylight," I said. "Have a good evening, Grandmother White Hail. See you later, Junior."

A little while later, as I approached our family land, I saw the black Model T parked on the hill above our house. *Do they have their guns pointed at me? Should I turn around and make a run for it? Should I race home and warn my grandfather?*

Gunfire rang out. *Pop! Pop! Pop!* . . . Three shots!

Surprise Encounter

M y first instinct was to turn around and head back toward Aunt Pearl's. But then another memory found its way into my thoughts: my father telling me to be a man, to face my fears.

I grabbed my rifle and rode as fast as I could toward home. I hoped everyone was safe.

First thing I did when I got home was put Chepa on the back porch and give him some water. Next, I looked around all the corrals for Grandfather. I found him shoeing horses, pretending not to notice the commotion above us on the hill. I knew the gunshots bothered him as much as it did me. I tried not to dwell on my fears, but Superintendent O'Neil's intimidation was getting harder to live with. Something was going to give soon. I felt it in my bones.

Grandfather motioned toward the hill with his mouth. "Grandchild, don't worry about them. We need to stay on the bright side of things. Sure, the fire they started destroyed our crops and haystacks, but at the same time, it burned away plant debris and dead trees. The burned land can make way for healthy vegetation to thrive. If we trench a few ditches from Medicine Creek into our land, I believe we will survive this."

It was hard to look on the bright side when we had to listen to occasional gunfire.

I felt it was time to tell Grandfather about the land papers I found and my visit with Aunt Pearl.

I expected to hear a lecture from Grandfather about keeping secrets from him, but he commended me on my courage and called me a very brave young man.

Grandfather said, "If anyone knows what to do with the papers, my sister-in-law Pearl is the one."

I explained to Grandfather, "She knows a young man named Lone Feather who is going to school at South Dakota State College. His English name is Benjamin Reifel. He has a deep interest in putting a stop to illegal land grabs like Superintendent O'Neil is trying to do to us. She said he might be able to help, and she was going to talk to him."

Grandfather said, "Oh-ha, that will be good."

The delicious aroma of rabbit stew and Lakota fry bread wafted toward us from the cabin. Grandfather stood up and rubbed his hands together. "Now! Let's go eat."

The wind shifted, and everything went dark. A sharp boot kick in my ribs brought me around. I was yanked upright into a sitting position. My hands and feet were tied together at the wrists and ankles.

"Stand up, old man!" a muffled voice commanded. It sounded like the voice of Jess Miller.

Grandfather said, "You two better move on. You have no place here."

"You don't say?" said the voice of the other man. I recognized his voice as belonging to Big Jim.

I could hear a scuffle, and I tried to turn my head enough to see Grandfather from the corner of my eye. I felt helpless.

Jess Miller said, "I am sure the Plenty Buffalo family would give anything for the safe return of their old man, even land. Ha ha!"

"I second that fact!" It sounded like Superintendent O'Neil walking up from behind the barn. "Load him up, and let's be on our way. Time is short!"

Helplessly listening to the sound of horse hooves fading off in the distance, I knew Grandfather was in deep trouble.

I struggled to free myself but was tied up tight. I spied a hoe leaned up against the side of the barn. I inched closer and closer until I reached the hoe. After knocking it to the ground, I worked the ropes tying my wrists against the blade of the hoe. The rope frayed into weak strands and finally unraveled. With no time to waste, I freed myself and ran toward the cabin.

As soon as I opened the back porch screen door, Chepa started to bark. He sensed danger in the air and was in a frenzy.

I told Grandmother and Mother, "Superintendent O'Neil and his goons jumped us in the corral, and they took Grandfather. I am going to Uncle Jay's to get help. Keep Chepa inside until I get back."

I packed my rifle and water in my saddlebags. I jumped on Anpo and galloped down the dusty road to rescue my grandfather.

I quickly told Uncle Jay what had happened. We rode our horses to the bend near the stickball field and picked up Harvey Two Crow, Orson, and Junior White Hail. We followed the shallow hoofprints southwest into the Dry Creek ravine. Uncle Jay could tell there were four horses.

After about two miles into the ravine, Uncle Jay said, "I think I know where they might be. Years ago, I went fishing with my uncle Jack at Catfish Creek. There is an abandoned homestead on the east side of the creek; the barn has fallen over, but the sod house is still standing. I believe James O'Neil and his boys have Thomas holed up there. The abandoned homestead is about five miles ahead at the mouth of this ravine."

Uncle Jay shouted, "Let's go! A life is at stake!"

We rode at a full gallop toward Catfish Creek.

The sod house was well hidden, tucked into a steep concave bluff. It was almost invisible unless you looked twice. It was made of prairie sod and dried grass. The roof that once grew food for the family was covered with overgrown shrubs.

We tied the horses as far away as possible and quietly crept closer, keeping to the shadows.

The front of the cabin faced west, and the door was wide open. By the scuff marks on the ground in front of the cabin, we knew there had been a tussle.

Orson, Junior, and I hid behind a thicket of wild plum bushes. Orson whispered, "Hey, Alfred, I can see your grandfather."

The light inside the sod house was dim. I could barely make out the outline of a man, but I was sure it was Grandfather. He sat on the dirt floor with his hands tied behind his back at the wrists. Jess Miller sat next to Grandfather, holding his rifle close and ready for action.

Uncle Jay motioned for me to go around to the south side of the sod house and for Orson, Junior, and Harvey to go around to the north side. I inched closer and closer, almost to the open window.

"Where do you think you're going, boy?" A gun barrel jammed me in the back. It was Big Jim! He pushed me forward toward the open door.

Showdown at Catfish Creek

P ut that rifle down! Now!" he yelled.
I dropped my rifle on the ground next to my feet.

Big Jim punched my shoulder with the butt end of his rifle. I fell, facedown, and lay there sprawled in the dirt with his boot on my back and his gun pointed at my head.

"Boy, if you had a lick of sense, you'd stayed put where we left you."

Big Jim pulled a rope out of his back pocket and tied my hands behind my back. He pushed me through the open doorway. Grandfather tried to stand up when he saw me, but Jess Miller knocked him back down.

A shadowy figure stepped through the open door, immersed in the bright afternoon sunlight. The silhouette walked toward Grandfather and swung an object in the air. *Whack!* Grandfather slumped to the dirt floor. It was Superintendent

O'Neil holding a broken wooden chair leg he used as a club.

I struggled to break free to help Grandfather, but Big Jim gave me a painful kick, knocking me into the dirt next to Grandfather.

Superintendent O'Neil stood above us, rubbing his hands together. "My, my, what do we have here? This might just be one of the luckiest days of my life. The old man and his wimpy grandson. I am getting two birds with one stone."

At that moment, Uncle Jay, Orson, Junior, and Harvey stormed through the door and tackled Jess Miller and Big Jim.

"Put your guns down or I will shoot the boy in the head." Superintendent O'Neil stood above me with his Colt .45 pressed against my temple. I rammed my knee up into Superintendent O'Neil's groin, and with a moan, he slumped forward. As he fell, he fired a random shot into the crumbling ceiling above. Harvey twisted O'Neil's arm behind his back and tied his hands together at the wrists.

Jess Miller made a dash for the rifle but wasn't quick enough. Orson landed an uppercut on Miller's chin before he could reach the rifle. Jess went down cold. Uncle Jay jumped Big Jim from behind. The two went down in a fury of moans, groans, and dust.

Uncle Jay kept Big Jim pinned down while Junior tied him up with a rope.

"Orson! Junior! Go get the horses so we can get these crooks back to Iron Nation before we lose our daylight," Uncle Jay shouted.

Harvey untied us. It took a moment for Grandfather to sit up. Even bruised and bloody, he was able to walk.

Grandfather pointed at the canvas canteen near the wall. "Grandchild, pass me that canteen so I can get a drink of water. I'm about as parched as a pile of coyote bones on the prairie."

I handed Grandfather the canteen, relieved to hear his voice.

Uncle Jay found a canvas bag hanging on a nail behind the door. He brought the bag into the light for a better look. Uncle Jay rummaged through the loot.

He said, "Looks like a stack of stolen and forged lease papers, checks, and money. A good bag of evidence, if you ask me."

Orson and Junior returned with the horses. Superintendent O'Neil was tied to the saddle behind Uncle Jay. Orson carried Jess Miller, and Harvey, Big Jim. Grandfather rode with me, and Junior kept watch at the rear.

We rode in silence, and when we reached the outskirts of Iron Nation, the sun was setting below the clouds in the western sky.

"Woof, woof, woof." Chepa announced our arrival.

Grandmother and Mother met us at the gate and ran to help Grandfather down. "I was so worried, Thomas. I prayed Great Spirit would bring all of you home safely. He did, and I am grateful beyond words."

Grandfather hugged her tenderly, and turning to us, he said, "Take those crooks to the barn, and make darn sure they are tied up good. We will take shifts keeping them guarded through the night."

Harvey said, "Thomas, I'll keep watch until midnight, and maybe Jay can take over then."

Uncle Jay agreed.

"I will send Jim Yellow Hair to the agency tonight to notify the Tribal police," Grandfather said.

"At first light in the morning, we will escort them and their stolen goods to Lower Brule Agency."

Junior shook my hand. "Friend Alfred, I am glad I could help out today. I wish I could stay longer, but it's dark and I need to get home. I am sure my grandmother is worried about me right about now."

Orson couldn't resist. "Hey, Junior, you sure did a good job knuckling Big Jim's head today. Reminded me of the days you used to practice on Alfred. Hee-hee."

I jumped in. "Junior and I had a good talk. That is all behind us now. We have many great adventures ahead as friends."

Junior nodded his affirmation. Orson liked that and gave us both his dazzling smile. My friends headed home, and I headed inside, beat-down tired.

Grandmother and Grandfather were seated at the kitchen table, quietly talking over coffee.

Grandfather said, "Have a good sleep, Grandchild. I am sure dawn will come soon enough."

I replied, "Thank you, Grandfather. I will."

My dreams were troubling, and I woke up in the morning feeling on edge.

Passing Grandfather on my way to the outhouse, I was taken aback by his worried face.

I said, "What's wrong, Grandfather?"

He said, "Grandchild, I have bad news. Superintendent O'Neil, Jess Miller, and Big Jim escaped during the night. Jay showed up at midnight to relieve Harvey from his guard, and he found Harvey tied up with a rag in his mouth. I told Harvey and Jay we will look for tracks and signs as soon as we get good light."

I asked Grandfather, "Did they get the stolen money and goods that we confiscated as evidence?"

Grandfather said, "No, we still have all the evidence. I am sorry, grandchild, to have to give you such grim news."

I asked, "Did anyone let Aunt Pearl know what happened?"

Grandfather said, "Yes, your grandmother sent her nephew Sam to inform Pearl. Pearl told Sam to tell us that she will contact Benjamin Reifel today to start legal proceedings against Superintendent O'Neil and his men. She also said that Benjamin will notify the capital police in Pierre today to be on the lookout for them, since Jess Miller has family in Fort Pierre."

I thought about James O'Neil, Jess Miller, and Big Jim still being on the loose. My spirit stone moved against my chest, and I felt the quiver of danger inside.

I thought, *We will never be safe if they are around.*

Time Will Tell

I packed everything I thought we needed and even some extra gear. Grandfather and I met up with Harvey Two Crow and Uncle Jay at the crossroad. Orson and Junior White Hail soon joined us. Orson and I tried hard to keep from teasing Junior at the sight of his chinks, or leggings, that covered his legs to the kneecap. Each chink was made of thick lambswool and looked very hot and uncomfortable.

Orson, unable to resist a good poke, said, "Where'd you get those fancy lambskins?"

Junior answered, "My grandfather gave them to me before he passed. He said I would grow into them someday, and here I am."

Orson laughed. "Looks like you're riding a sheep. Hope we don't run into a pack of hungry wolves."

Grandfather hid his smile. "Now, boys. Let's go!"

113

We all knew how dangerous it was for us to leave our Lakota reservation without passes and to be in hot pursuit of three runaway white men. I touched my spirit stone and prayed that Aunt Pearl would hold to her end of the deal.

From the bluff, we saw a group of Lakota women patiently lined up in the center of a large camp of tepees and army tents below. It was monthly ration day, and I was sure Grandmother was in line, holding her paper ration ticket. When the federal government agent opened the side of the box tent, the women scurried about to collect their rations of beef, salt, beans, corn, flour, and sometimes coffee, sugar, and tobacco. But, as good as it sounds, the flour and corn were always infested with weevils and mold. And the beef was often rotten.

We rode on, and ten miles west of Iron Nation, Uncle Jay pointed to a red bandana stuck on a berry bush and hoofprints that veered off on a different path toward Cedar Creek. Uncle Jay jumped off his horse to get a closer look.

"We're on their trail, boys," he said. "This is old Big Jim's bandana. They must have picked up three horses somewhere. Looks like they are headed toward Fort Pierre. It's going to be about a thirty-five-mile run for us. Let's give our horses some water and a break and get a bite to eat."

We followed Uncle Jay toward a spring that was not too far from the trail. Rested and nourished from the dried deer pemmican and water, we mounted up and continued westward.

About ten miles southeast of Fort Pierre, the late afternoon sun turned a deep crimson, and the wind picked up.

Uncle Jay shouted, "Dust blizzard! We need to find shelter fast!" Pointing north, he said, "There's a log cabin over the hill about a quarter of a mile. We can stay there until the storm clears!"

We galloped down a steep trail adjacent to the river. Just when I feared we would lose sight of one another, a cabin loomed through the brown wall of dust.

Harvey and Uncle Jay went ahead of us toward the cabin. Orson, Junior, and I followed Grandfather around the east side to secure our horses in a sheltered grove of trees. Still struggling against the wind, Grandfather and I managed to make it to the cabin door. Orson and Junior were not far behind us.

I burst through the door. "Hey, Uncle Jay! Did you—"

I froze in my tracks.

"Drop your guns, boys!" a familiar voice commanded.

In the dimness, I could faintly see Harvey tied up and slumped against the far corner wall. Uncle Jay sat upright on the dirt floor, tied up as well.

"O'Neil!" Grandfather gasped.

"Well, heck, old man, seems like we've been down this road before. I think we have some unfinished business to settle."

O'Neil's fist connected with Grandfather just as Orson and Junior stormed in. Orson rolled to the right and I to the left, Junior to the right. The skirmish confused O'Neil long enough for Grandfather to wrestle free.

O'Neil pulled the trigger as Grandfather knocked the gun from his hand. The stray bullet hit Big Jim and wedged in his abdomen. Grandfather's fist connected with O'Neil's chin, and he was out cold.

"Ahhh, I'm shot," Big Jim moaned as he crumpled to the floor.

Jess Miller plunged toward O'Neil's gun that was lying on the dirt floor, but Junior jumped on Jess Miller's back and pinned him down.

Grandfather picked up a rope from the dirt floor and threw it at Orson. "Quickly! Tie up Miller and O'Neil. Grandson, untie Jay and Harvey!"

All eyes turned toward Big Jim, who lay sprawled faceup. A puddle of blood seeped out from under his still body, getting bigger and bigger. Grandfather bent over him to feel his pulse. There was nothing. "He's dead."

When the storm cleared, I stepped outside for some fresh air. I took a deep breath and let the fresh air fill my lungs and steady my emotions. Grandfather followed me outside and took out his tobacco pouch. He rolled himself a cigarette, offered a short prayer, and sprinkled tobacco on the ground for Big Jim's journey.

Grandfather turned to me and said, "We're going on to Fort Pierre. Big Jim's corpse won't keep for very long in the heat of the day. Best we travel while it's cool."

We found the stolen horses not too far from the cabin. Grandfather draped Big Jim's corpse over one of the horses, and O'Neil and Jess Miller, their hands tightly secured, were mounted on the other two. We tied the three horses to our saddle horns and took our prisoners toward Fort Pierre. There was no need to talk; we rode in silence under a bright blue moon.

When we reached Fort Pierre, we took our prisoners straight to the brick courthouse that also served as a jail. Hearing our horses, Deputy Sheriff John Riggs met us on the walkway, carrying a kerosene lantern. He was surprised to see a dead man draped over a horse and six wide-eyed Natives mounted on horseback. He hesitated to move closer.

Grandfather called out, "John, it's me, Thomas Plenty Buffalo. We have something for you."

Deputy Riggs stepped toward us. "Thomas, I sure didn't recognize you. What do you have here? By gollies, you rounded up old James O'Neil and his sidekicks. We got word today they were on the loose. By the looks of it, one of them is shot dead. Bring the two live ones inside. Leave the corpse out here. I'll call the undertaker to come over and pick him up."

"Deputy Riggs, we also have quite a bit of evidence that needs to be turned over to your office," Grandfather explained.

Deputy Sheriff Riggs replied, "Yes, I know. Mr. Benjamin Reifel and Mrs. Pearl Hand were here earlier this afternoon. They let us know everything that happened and told us that if we had any questions, to contact them at Mr. Reifel's office."

I thought to myself, *Good, I knew Lone Feather and Aunt Pearl would keep their word and not let us down!*

We circled out of town and back toward the river before someone asked to see a traveling permit that we didn't have. We picked up the pace, anxious to make camp and get some shut-eye. The ride gave me a moment to ponder. Fortunately for us, it appeared to be the end of a land-grab scheme from a crooked agency superintendent. Unfortunately, the Native land grabs would keep going on until someone in authority put a stop to it. I smiled inside. I sure wouldn't quit having my spirit dreams or adventures. And I darn sure wouldn't stop believing my father would come home someday. I just hoped the next superintendent would be a better man and not worse. Only time would tell.

lfreda Beartrack-Algeo is a storyteller and poet as well as an artist and illustrator. She is a member of the Lower Brule Lakota Nation, Kul Wicasa Oyate, Lower Brule, South Dakota, where she grew up surrounded by her extended family, her circle of family and friends. Alfreda uses various art forms to tell her stories. Alfreda says, "It is a very sensitive and beautiful experience to be a storyteller. There is a story in everything I create, from the smallest rock to the mightiest mountain. With every character born, every story shared, I add a piece of my spirit to this great matrix of life. As long as I have a story left to tell, I feel I have a responsibility to gift that story forward." Alfreda currently lives in beautiful Palisade, Colorado, with her spouse, David Algeo.

PathFinders novels offer exciting contemporary and historical stories featuring Native teens and written by Native authors. For more information, visit NativeVoicesBooks.com.

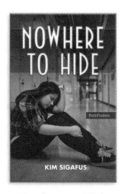

Nowhere to Hide
Kim Sigafus
978-1-939053-21-3 • $9.95

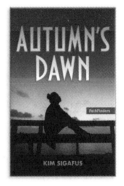

Autumn's Dawn
Kim Sigafus
978-1-939053-25-1 • $9.95

Finding Grace
Kim Sigafus
978-1-939053-29-9 • $9.95